Notes From the Midnight Driver

JORDAN SONNENBLICK

SCHOLASTIC INC.

New York   Toronto   London   Auckland   Sydney
Mexico City   New Delhi   Hong Kong   Buenos Aires

This book was originally published in hardcover by Scholastic Press in 2006.

ISBN-13: 978-0-439-75781-2
ISBN-10: 0-439-75781-9

13 12 11 10 9 8   9 10 11 12/0

Printed in the U.S.A.   40
First Scholastic paperback printing, October 2007

The text type was set in Gill Sans.
The display type was set in Chauncy DeluxxeBold.
Book design by Marijka Kostiw

To my grandfather,

Solomon Feldman,

who inspired this book,

and to the memory of my father,

Dr. Harvey Sonnenblick,

who loved it

Boop. *Boop. Boop.*

I'm sitting next to the old man's bed, watching the bright green line spike and jiggle across the screen of his heart monitor. Just a couple of days ago, those little mountains on the monitor were floating from left to right in perfect order, but now they're jangling and jerking like maddened hand puppets.

I know that sometime soon, the boops will become one long beep, the mountains will crumble into a flat line, and I will be finished with my work here.

I will be free.

GNOME RUN

It seemed like a good idea at the time. Yes, I know everybody says that — but I'm serious. As insane as it looks in retrospect, I was fully convinced on that particular Friday evening last September that stealing my mom's car and storming my dad's house was a brilliant plan. And not brilliant, as in, "That was a brilliant answer you gave in Spanish today." I mean brilliant, as in, "Wow, Einstein, when you came up with that relativity thing, and it revolutionized our entire concept of space and time while also leading all of humankind into the nuclear age, that was brilliant!"

The plan had a certain elegant simplicity, too. I would drink one more pint of Dad's old vodka, grab Mom's spare car keys, jump into the Dodge, and fire that sucker up. Then I would speed through the deserted, moonlit streets, straight and true as a homing missile, or at least straight and true as a sober person who actually knew how to drive. When I skidded triumphantly into Dad's driveway, I would leap nimbly from the car, race to the front door, ring the bell with a fury rarely encountered by any bell, anywhere — and catch my father with the no-good home-wrecking wench who was once, in a forgotten life we used to have, my third-grade teacher.

Okay, perhaps these plans would theoretically work better if the planner were not already completely intoxicated. But I'd never gotten drunk before — so how was I supposed to know I'd get so smashed so quickly? And hey, if my mom had really wanted to keep me from driving drunk without a license at age sixteen, would she have gone out on a date and left me home with a car, a liquor cabinet, and some keys?

I rest my case.

So I downed some more booze straight from the bottle and lunged for the key ring, grabbing it by the wooden number 1 I had made for my "Number One Mom" in Cub Scouts. I threw on my Yankees jacket, slammed my way out of the house, got into the car, and started it. Then I believe there was some drama with the gear stick and the parking brake, and probably a bit of fun with the gas pedal.

The next thing I knew, I was hanging out the passenger door, puking up vodka and Ring Dings. When I got my eyes sort of focused, I could see that the car was up on a lawn. When I got them even more focused, I could see that my last salvo of vomit had completely splattered two shiny black objects — the well-polished shoes of one angry police officer. He yanked me out of the car, largely by the hair, and stood me up. I remember him saying, "Look at that! Look what you did." I also remember trying to follow his pointing finger. And when I finally zoomed in on what was lying in front of the car, I couldn't believe it. There was a detached head about ten feet in front of the bumper!

The cop sort of puppet-marched me up to the horrific scene and forced *my* head down close to the carnage. This head was seriously injured, to be sure. It was upside down, smushed up against a tree stump. There was no body in sight. I whirled around so fast that the cop almost lost hold of me, and crouched to look under Mom's car. Sure enough, an arm and a leg were sticking out from underneath the left front wheel.

"Officer, sir, did I — is he — is — ummm . . ."

I could feel the tears welling up. My eyes burned, and the next wave of acid was coming up my throat in a hurry.

"Yes, son. You ruined my brand-new shoes, smashed up your car, and decapitated Mrs. Wilson's French lawn gnome. You're in some serious . . ."

"Lawn gnome? LAWN GNOME?"

Now that I looked a bit more closely, I noticed that the head wasn't bleeding, and that the ear had cracked off with inhuman neatness. I began to laugh like an idiot, but my relief came too late to halt my barf, which came out mostly through my nose — and landed on the officer's left side, all over his walkie-talkie.

This was even more of a crack-up. I started

mumbling, "Walkie-talkie-barfie, walkie-talkie-barfie," which amused me almost all the way to the police station. You would think I'd have been pretty scared by this point, but because I had drunk so much vodka so fast, I was still getting drunker by the second. Even with my hands cuffed behind my back — and the cuffs were REALLY tight, because the officer hadn't been enjoying me much so far — I was like a little one-man house party in the back seat of the cruiser. The last thing I remember was getting bored of the dispatch radio, and shouting, "Change the station! Get me some ROCK!" Then the car turned a sharp corner, and the window was tilting and rushing toward my face.

You know what must really be a highlight of being a desk cop? Processing the arrests of drunk people. After several of my new pals in blue dragged me semiconscious (I mean, I was semiconscious; they were pretty alert) into the station, they left me cuffed to a scuffed-up old wooden seat across from some old guy with a badge. I decided his name was

Sarge. He had that fingerprinting pad thing and a bunch of questions for me, and didn't waste any time easing into things.

"Right thumb."

I stared at the weaving, bobbing blurs that had replaced my hands, trying to figure out which was which. "I can't find the right one; they're too bloody."

Sure enough, they were, because I had a cut over my left eye, which must have been hidden from view beneath my adorable mop of hair. Sarge apparently saw the blood, but not the source, because he sighed one of those big annoyed sighs that public servants make when they are forced to do actual work, reached into his desk, and pulled out a pack of wet wipes. "Geez, you must'a really banged your nose. Get your hands cleaned up, kid. I'll be back in a minute. By the way, genius, your right hand is the one that ain't chained to the desk."

He walked away to get a cup of coffee or whatever. I got my hands clean, then reached my free hand up to wipe the hair out of my eyes. Which got it all gory again. I repeated this at least three times, creating an impressive pile of crumbled, deep-pink-stained wipes. Then I got the marvy idea that maybe I could just wipe the blood off my head first. I pushed my hair all the way up off my forehead, the alcohol-soaked wipe touched my wound, and I sobered up REAL fast, just as Sarge was putting his cup of steaming liquid on the desk blotter.

"Ooooowwwww!" I screamed. Up I jumped. Up jumped my arm. Up jumped the handcuff. Up jumped the desk. Up flew the coffee.

"Ooooowwwww!" screamed Sarge. Sarge was wet!

Eventually the sodden mass of paper, blood, wipes, and coffee was disposed of by a guy in rubber gloves. Sarge found a new pair of pants, and came back. He took a really long look at my forehead, the mixture of blood, snot, and tears that was flowing freely across my facial features, and the moist abstract painting that had been his desk blotter, and decided to use a trick which always works for my dad: He would make me Somebody Else's Problem.

Sarge shouted across the room, "Call me an ambulance!"

I couldn't stop myself. "Okay, you're an ambulance!"

And so it went, until the paramedics accidentally banged my head against the doorway of the emergency room, and I passed out for good.

THE WAKE-UP

The next morning, I had two new experiences, and they both hurt. I had never woken up with a hangover or a concussion before, but —WHOA!— I guess there's a first time for everything.

Before I opened my gummy, grainy eyes, a shadow crossed over me. I begged it for help. "Sarge, Sarge, can I please have some water? Water, please? Oh, God, WATER!"

It replied so sweetly that I knew who it was without looking. "Good morning, Alex. Congratulations. You got arrested and ruined everybody's night. The car is in bad shape, too. And who the hell is Sarge?"

"Hi, Mom," I croaked.

As I finally pried my eyelids open, the glare of the sun through the hospital room window almost made me faint. But before I could even lose consciousness in peace, Mom grabbed me in a rib-pulverizing body hug. "Oh, Alex. Oh, my baby!"

"Mom, I'm okay. Really," I gasped like a dying salmon.

She looked me dead in the eyes then, and wiped tears from the corners of hers. "You're not okay," she snapped. "You're an idiot!" Then she whacked me on the arm really hard, just as my father stampeded in.

While I was gingerly checking my bicep area for spurting arteries, Dad burst into high-volume mode. "Oh, good, Janet, why don't you just beat the boy to death while we're here? It will be convenient, with the morgue right downstairs and all."

"Don't 'Good, Janet' me, Simon. It's your fault the boy is lying here all . . . all . . . all . . ."

"Smacked?" I chimed in.

"Shut up!" they exclaimed in unison. See, divorced people CAN cooperate where the children are concerned.

"And how is this my fault? You leave him at your house, drunk, *with the car keys,* while you're gallivanting around town with some . . ."

"*I* leave him drunk?"

"Yes, *you* leave him drunk."

"*Whose* liquor is still at the house?"

"What do you mean, *still* at the house? It was *your* lawyer who said I couldn't remove any *common property* from the —"

I couldn't tolerate this Battle of the Italics any longer. I looked away and started picking at an itch on my left arm. My fingers encountered something alarming there — I was hooked up to an IV! What was THAT about? I needed to know, pronto, so I reached out for the button on the side of my bed, and desperately buzzed for help. A nurse came in, threaded her way between my still-raging parents, and stopped by my bedside with an expectant look and a question. "Hi, I'm Miss Anderson. I'll be your nurse today. What can I do for you?"

"Um, hi. My name is Alex and, uh, do you know why I have a needle in my arm? Am I, um, critically injured or anything? I mean, because I'd want to know that."

She sighed. "No, you're not critically injured, Alex. But from what your mother told me before you woke up, you're very lucky not to be."

I glanced over at my parents — they were both still going bonkers on each other, to the point where a casual bystander might have started looking for something to hide under in case they reached the "throwing-objects" stage. This wasn't my idea of a very lucky scenario, but whatever. "Yes, ma'am. I just want to know what's wrong with me."

My mom paused in her vicious attack on my father's parenting and general life skills to throw a jab my way: "Yes, Nurse. We'd love to know what's wrong with him, too."

Miss Anderson looked like an innocent Roman who had somehow walked onto the floor of the Coliseum right into the middle of a "Throwing-Christians-to-the-Lions" marathon. She was saved from answering, though, by the entrance of Dr. Friedman, or at least some guy wearing Dr. Friedman's badge. "Ah, Mr. Alexander Gregory, the famous midnight driver. I overheard your request, and I will be glad to tell you what's going on. I'd imagine you're feeling pretty rocky right now — is that correct?"

I nodded and tried to look pathetic, which came naturally at that moment.

"Well, there are several valid reasons for that. One, you came to us with a fairly significant case of alcohol poisoning. That's why your mouth and eyes are probably very dry: Alcohol poisoning causes dehydration. That's also why you have an intravenous line in your arm. Two, you sustained at least one strong blow to the head last night, possibly when your head hit the steering wheel of your mother's car. This caused your soft brain to bounce off of the hard inside of your cranium. So you have a concussion, which means that even if the drinking hadn't given you a pounding headache, dizziness, and nausea, you'd certainly have them now anyway. Three, you split your forehead open. It wasn't a deep gash, but it was fairly jagged, so we had to suture it up. A plastic surgeon will be by later today to check on the stitching job, and you can ask him how bad he thinks the scar might be."

Scar? Holy moley. That was cause for panic. But I didn't have time to think about it for long, because the doctor was still talking: "By the way, does your right shoulder ache?"

I hadn't singled out that one particular strand of discomfort in the thick rope of agony that was twisting around my brain, but, "Yes, it does. Why?"

"Tetanus shot. Do you have any specific questions I haven't covered?"

"Uh, can I get some kind of medicine for my head? It really hurts. Please?"

"We'll see what your next blood toxicology report shows, but right now I don't want to give your liver any additional work to do. You gave it quite a workout last night."

Great. Head trauma without painkillers. Now there's a recipe for wholesome fun.

After the doctor left, my mom announced that she needed some air, and stomped out with one last glare at my dad. Dad ambled over to the side of the bed and sort of punched my shoulder in a fatherly way — which would have been just peachy if he hadn't hit the exact spot my mother had already pulverized. Then, completely ignoring my gasp and wince, he gave me a whole big speech about responsibility while I closed my eyes and tried very hard not to picture him cheating on my mom with my third-grade teacher.

Eventually, I turned my head to the wall and pretended to be asleep — which he noticed after maybe seven or eight minutes. I swear, I almost let out a fake snore just to speed up the process, but was afraid it might make him shake me back to consciousness. It felt as though getting shaken might very well have made my head fall off, so I wasn't willing to take the risk.

I don't remember Dad leaving, so I must have fallen asleep for real at some point. Next thing I knew, Mom was sitting on the edge of the bed, holding my hand, and crying again. I gave an encore performance of my "slumbering boy" routine, only this time I was doing it for a different reason — I didn't want my mother to see that *my* eyes were welling up, too.

DAy OF THE DORK-WIT

I spent that whole day in the hospital, and went home on Sunday — right after a nice lady from Social Services came by to "release me into the custody of my parents." Before we left, my mom had to sign a whole bunch of police papers. She also had to promise to get me a lawyer and deliver me to court in thirty days for a hearing on my drunk-driving case. You didn't have to be a genius to realize this was going to be a long month.

Mom wasn't particularly speaking to me for most of the morning at home, but I was too sore to go out and do anything, so I spent hours in the basement noodling around on my electric guitar. It's the best thing I own, a real American Fender Telecaster with a beautiful sunburst finish that my dad bought me in a moment of guilt right after he moved out sophomore year. At the time I spent about twelve millionths of a second contemplating whether I should refuse to accept such a transparent bribe gift, but gimme a break — it was a Tele, and my old acoustic guitar from middle school was a cheap-o imported job. So I just told myself that living well is the best revenge, plugged the Tele in, and played for about a month nonstop.

Anyway, I took lessons until a couple of months after my parents separated, so I picked up a lot of the basics from my teacher. Then I quit the lessons because I figured *somebody* had to attempt to conserve my college fund in the face of my parents' rising legal bills. After that, I worked hard on figuring out the exercises from books and magazines, and kept playing in the high school jazz band. I wasn't a great jazz guitar player, because jazz is the hardest guitar music on the planet, but I could ROCK. So there I was, raging along with a pile of CDs with my little amp cranked, until I got really woozy. Then I turned the amp way down, turned the CD player off, and did some finger exercises and scales until the nausea and boredom became too overwhelming. I knew I couldn't stay down in the basement until my mom forgot all about my little automotive adventure, so I trudged up for lunch.

There she was at the table, dipping a biscotti into a cup of coffee over and over without taking a bite. She looked up and pointed the soggy baked good at my chest, dripping brown semiliquid goo everywhere. "Alex, I've been sitting here for hours, listening to you play, and trying to understand something. Do you know what I can't figure out?"

She waited so long I started to worry that maybe the question wasn't rhetorical.

"I can't figure out WHY you got drunk and took my car. Where were you trying to go, besides Mrs. Wilson's azalea bush? You're a smart boy, but this is just . . . stupid and pointless."

I suppose that I could have told her about my boffo plan to bum-rush her ex's house, but the whole separation thing wasn't something that got discussed much at our table. "I dunno, Mom. I just wanted to DO something. You were out having fun, I was stuck here alone, the computer wasn't working, and you TOOK my phone away last month, if you recall, so what was I supposed to do? Study precalc on a Friday night? Invite over some other loveless, unpopular dork to play Nintendo? Organize the bathroom cabinet?"

"Well, you could have . . ."

Aha, she was on the defensive. As soon as you get your mom out of attack mode, you're home free. "Could have what?"

"I don't know, Alex — but almost anything would have been better than what you actually DID. What if you had KILLED someone?"

Okay, maybe she wasn't quite ready to lay down her guns.

"Mom, I didn't kill anyone. I didn't even hurt anyone. I broke a stupid garden-elf thing. I should probably be getting a reward for making the neighborhood more tasteful, for God's sake. And I wasn't even trying to do anything bad. I just wanted to go to Dad's house and yell at him for leaving *you*!" So much for avoiding the separation topic.

"You were trying to go to Dad's? *That's* what

you were trying to do? But you didn't even make it to the end of the block!"

"Mistakes were made, Mom. Is that what you want me to say? Mistakes were made."

"Yes, mistakes were made, Alex. Like me trusting you, that was a biggie. Now let me tell you how things are going to be for the next month until your court date. You will be driven to school by ME, you will be picked up at school by ME, you will do your homework the instant you get home in front of ME, and then you will engage in quiet activities IN THE HOUSE until bedtime at ten P.M."

Ten P.M.?

"Mom, how are you going to drop me off, pick me up, get to work on time, and sleep?" Mom is a night-shift nurse at an old people's home, so she usually slept while I was at school.

"I don't know, Alex. I will have to work something out, because I am going to be on you like a bad rash for the next thirty days. And if you don't like it, maybe you should have thought about that BEFORE you got arrested."

Just then, I tried to brush back the hair that was falling over my eyes as I slumped down at the table. A searing pain slashed along the stitches in my forehead and my head jerked forward. Instantly tears sprang to my eyes.

"Oh, Alex, did that hurt?"

I sniffled. "Yeah, Mom."

"GOOD!"

Obviously, home was somewhat tense. So I thought school on Monday would actually be a relief for once. Which might have been true, if every single kid in the building hadn't somehow turned into a fanatical newshound over the weekend. In the hallway that first day, most people just looked at me quickly, sideways, and then looked away to avoid staring at my bruised face and zigzag of black stitches. But there's always some weasel that just can't let things go, right? When I got to homeroom, my weasel struck.

"Whoa, look, it's Harry Potter! That scar is a great look for you, Gregory. Really. Who does your makeup, and can you get me an appointment for — oh, I don't know — never?" It was Bryan Gilson, the most obnoxious guy in the junior class. It used to be, back in middle school, that we were all constantly busting on each other. But somehow, Bryan hadn't quite noticed when everybody else grew out of it. Plus, his dad was a police officer, so it figured that he would have the whole lowdown on my situation. I tried to walk past him to my seat without saying anything.

"Hey, don't worry, it could be worse. Sure you look bad, but you should see the other guy. Or GNOME, I should say."

I took a deep breath. Two. Three. Sat down in my seat. Bryan walked over and stood next to me. Everyone was staring now, naturally, waiting to see whether I would jump up and try to slug Bryan. Who weighed about three hundred pounds more than me and played football, just in case my concussion, head wound, and crippling soreness weren't enough of an advantage for him. Just as the standoff was becoming unbearable, just when I would have had to say or do something, my best friend, Laurie Flynn, came streaking into the classroom. She ran over and pushed Gilson out of the way like he was a toddler. Yay! Laurie was here to deliver me from evil, to smite my enemies, to . . .

"Move it, siddown, and shut up, Bryan. Just because you're a hulking water buffalo doesn't mean I can't waste you with one hand tied behind my back like I did in third grade. And close your mouth before you drool on my shoes, you cretin!"

Then she actually TURNED HER BACK on Bryan, knowing he would slink away from her wrath. Of course, that meant all ninety-three pounds of her was suddenly focused on me. Before I could attempt to calm her down with a "thank-you," she leaned over with her forearms on my desk and let me have it.

Geez, where are homeroom teachers when you need 'em?

"Alex Peter Gregory, you are a moron." She slammed her palms down on my desk and stomped her foot.

I get a lot of that.

"You are a bonehead. You are a complete

goober. You're worse than a goober. You're like . . . an assistant goober! You're a dork, a half-wit. You're a . . . a . . . a dork-wit!"

I gave her a cheesy little puppy-dog face, but nothing was going to slow this steamroller down. "Please don't yell at me, Laurie. I'm in pain here, and you're not helping. Plus, everyone's staring at us. And, uh, you're standing on my foot."

She gave me the same demonic grin that she'd once used to make a substitute teacher quit in the middle of sixth-grade music class, and said, "I know."

"Well, do you think you could get off my toes for a minute and let me explain?"

"Oh, your mom explained everything, buddy boy. Didn't she tell you I called on Saturday, four times? And then again yesterday, twice? She must have gotten tired of telling me you 'just couldn't come to the phone,' because she finally gave in and told me the whole ugly, pathetic story while you were downstairs goofing around on your guitar."

A brief bit of explanation, here: Laurie is only

five feet tall, and looks exactly like Tinker Bell from Peter Pan. She has perfect blond hair, a little upturned button nose, sparkly blue eyes, a sweet little angel mouth, and even slightly pointy little elf ears — plus a perfect gymnast body that the other girls are always giving her dirty looks over. All of which she hates. So she takes karate three nights a week, including a special class in Chinese hand-weapon combat, wears nothing but baggy black clothes, and has three rings in her left eyebrow.

She still looks like a pixie — but she looks like a terrifying Goth pixie.

One other key fact about Laurie: Ever since she moved here from New York City when we were six, she has been pretty much my only friend. Oh, yeah, and my mom loves her. She's like the daughter Mom never had, but would have liked very much if God hadn't given her a dorky, uncoordinated nerdball of a son instead.

"I wasn't goofing around, I was practicing. What was I supposed to do, sit in the kitchen and let my mom beat me with a wooden spoon all day?"

"And why didn't you call me on Friday night if you were planning to do something so half-witted?"

"Laurie, I wasn't *planning* to do something half-witted."

"I suppose with your fantastic natural gift for it, who needs planning?"

"Ha-ha. Look, you weren't home on Friday night, remember? You were working at the Gap."

"Oh, that's right — stores don't have phones. And you've only known my cell number for half a decade, so you couldn't possibly get in touch with me that way."

"Okay, maybe I didn't *want* to call you, Miss Understanding Friend of the Year. I didn't want to get lectured, I wanted to get drunk. And face my dad. Instead of just sitting there all worried about . . ."

"About what? Whether the police might be getting bored without an idiot to arrest?"

"About my mom's first date, okay?"

Laurie actually stopped and thought about this for a moment. And the bell rang for first period.

My DAy IN COURT

Thirty days is a long time. I mean, it's not a long time if you're sitting and watching a glacier move, or if you're waiting for a chunk of radioactive uranium to become a safe material for jewelry-making. But it's an eternity if you're doing nothing but going to school, cranking out homework, and pacing around the house bickering with your mom. I was avoiding pretty much all human contact, with a special focus on ignoring my dad's attempts to communicate with me. He called daily, but I let the machine pick up, and then erased the increasingly pathetic messages. He e-mailed TWICE a day, but I never opened the files, and then I blocked him with my spam filter. Too bad my life didn't come with one of those; I would have been able to screen out his very existence. My parents didn't have a whole official custody thing worked out, partly because I was already sixteen, and partly because, like I said before, their divorce lawyers were too busy milking them for my college money to get the legal stuff finalized. But unofficially, my dad was supposed to be able to see me whenever he wanted.

Of course, he was also supposed to have stayed with my mom until death did them part, but we all know how that turned out. So if he could dump us, I could delete him like one of those suspicious e-mails from Africa where they ask for your bank account number.

I was more mixed up about why I was ducking Laurie at every turn. She could have listened, and maybe even given me some advice, or helped me figure out why I had basically nuked my life on a random Friday evening. Plus, her parents had been divorced since her sixth birthday party, when her mom hadn't showed, and her dad had stood up and announced that Daddy's "special present" for his little princess was going to be a real, live suburban dream home for two. So she knew the ropes, for sure.

But I kept remembering this time when we were

nine. I can see it now: I was wearing my pin-striped Yankees bathing suit. I had set up a skateboard ramp on the roof of my back porch, and a trampoline on the patio next to the pool. It seemed totally realistic to me that I could climb up onto the roof with my hot-green board, zip off the ramp, kick the board away in midair, bounce off the trampoline, and finish the stunt with a perfectly executed swan dive into the pool. I called her up and told her to rush over RIGHT NOW with her suit and her dad's video camera — this would be a moment that should be preserved for posterity, I figured.

So Laurie got there a few minutes later, took one look at my spectacular and well-planned-out setup, and immediately started trying to talk me out of the entire escapade. I can still hear her little pip-squeak voice echoing off the bricks of the patio: "Alex, this is dumb. A billion thousand things could go wrong."

"Duh, that's not even a real number. Plus, this is totally safe. I planned it SCIENTIFICALLY (my big word that summer, like when I had SCIENTIFICALLY spilled honey on a bees' nest to see whether they would die of happiness. The emergency-room doctors were getting lots of overtime thanks to my selfless devotion to SCIENCE). What could possibly happen?"

"Well, you could fall off the board on the roof, tumble off the roof, and die. Or you could make the jump, land on your board on the trampoline, and die. If you're better at this than I think you are, you might make the trampoline jump, then miss the pool, and die. Or make it into the pool, but hit your head on the edge, and die."

I admit, that last one was a pretty good guess.

The following September, the video became a truly legendary show-and-tell, but Laurie has never been one for looking on the bright side where my adventures are concerned. Which, again, is why I wasn't in a rush to consult with her on this latest escapade.

Anyway, between school, mom-time, and the big excitement of meeting with my lawyer (who is also my uncle Larry; his only comment was, "You really

SAID and DID all this?"), the month passed. And I got my day in court.

• • •

You wake up in the morning on your court date, and it's Showtime. You shower and shave the nine faint peach-fuzz follicles that may or may not yet exist on your face even though you tell your friends you have 'em. You brush, floss, brush again, gargle mouthwash, and still worry that you might get sent to jail due to bad breath. Your mom supervises you as you garb yourself for the battle in your only suit. Then you have to lean all the way forward as you eat your cornflakes so that no milk gets on your lovely baby-blue silk tie. Last spring's band-concert shoes go on; the blisters start. Your head buzzes with nervousness. Your palms are ice-cold and sweaty at the same time, which seems to defy all of the laws of nature, but whatever. Somehow, Mom shuffles you into the car, with its shiny new front bumper. The drive downtown is so quiet that you you can leave the radio off and just hear the sound waves directly through the frames of your sunglasses.

Mom parks three blocks from the courthouse, just so your blistering feet can really get some grind time in. The walk brings out more icy sweat, only this time it's all over your entire body. At the bottom of the marble courthouse steps, Mom gives you a quick hug, yanks off your sunglasses ("You don't want to look like a *criminal*!"), ruffles your hair like you're still five, and then tries to ruffle it back into neatness, even though you fully realize that if any aspect of your hygiene is going to get you sent to the slammer, it will still probably be the breath and not the comb & curl.

You wait in line, go through the metal detectors, meet your lawyer at the door of the courtroom, and walk in.

• • •

I was shocked when I first saw this particular courtroom, by the way. I had been expecting a big marble gallery-type room, with vaulted ceilings, dark wood everywhere, and maybe gargoyles of justice on top of Greek columns. But this place was just a tiny, plain box, with folding tables, which were for the defense and prosecutors, facing a metal desk. A smooth-looking old guy with greased-back hair and a suit so dark that it seemed to suck in the sickly fluorescent light was sitting sort of sideways in the prosecution chair, chatting with the judge and drinking coffee out of a paper Manhattan Bagel cup. He and my lawyer/uncle greeted each other like they worked together every day, which I guess they basically did. This was discouraging, though; I wanted my lawyer and the prosecutor to bare their teeth and snarl at each other, like gladiators entering the ring, not wave and nod like old college buddies.

If they were pals, who was on MY side?

The judge smiled at my mom. She was motherly looking, with dark hair tied in an old-fashioned bun, tiny black-framed glasses, and a regular gray business suit. Again, this was weird: Where was her robe? Where was her wooden hammer thing? And why was she saying, "Hello, Janet. I haven't seen you for a while. Still working at the home?"

Was this a court session, or a class reunion?

Before my mom could answer, the door swung open behind me, and things got a lot less chummy in a hurry. I was afraid to look anyone here in the eye, but I peeked sideways to see whose entry had clammed everybody up. Four guys in uniforms walked in. Two were paramedics, and two were familiar-looking police officers.

Oh, crud. These guys were my squad-car amigo and a guy who looked just like Sarge, only less blurry than I remembered him. Wow, this was enough to get me thinkin' about something my grandma had always said: *Be careful how you treat people, because you never know when you'll need their help later on.* And I hadn't exactly sown the seeds of love with these gents with all the spilling, laughing, and ralphing I'd done at our first encounter. Oh, and the underage drunk driving. Guess we shouldn't forget the under-age drunk driving.

We all sat down at the flimsy collapsible tables, and the judge started my big hearing, the most serious moment of my life to date. "Good morning, everybody. I've looked over the papers here, and in the case of New Jersey versus Alexander Gregory, the whole probable-cause *schtick* seems like a waste of time."

A waste of time? Was she just going to dismiss this whole thing, since everyone was in cahoots with each other anyway?

"Honestly, Mr. Sharpe (that would be Uncle Larry), this looks like a slam dunk."

Whoa, hold on a minute — SLAM DUNK? Shouldn't Uncle Larry be leaping up and shouting, "Objection?" The two officers were smirking, and the smoothie prosecutor was practically packing his briefcase already.

Uncle Larry leaped heroically to my defense, right after taking a big sip of coffee and flipping through his notes for ten seconds or so. "You're right, Judge. I know it's irregular, but since my client is a first offender, why don't we save everybody the time and expense of a trial and see what kind of plea we can figure out?"

Whoa, Unc. Way to stick up for the family honor.

The judge said, "Sounds good to me. Gentlemen?" She scanned the faces of the assorted 9-1-1 guys and prosecutor, all of whom now HAD started to get their things together. They were all mumbling and nodding, and suddenly the judge had the wood hammer dealie in her hand. "All righty, then. All rise." All rose. "In the case of New Jersey versus Alexander Gregory, the court accepts the defendant's guilty plea. The State of New Jersey will meet with the defendant for sentencing, right here, immediately following a fifteen-minute break." I couldn't stifle one panicky joke-thought: How were they going to get the whole state in this one little room?

Everyone except Uncle Larry, Mom, and I filed out the back door, making small talk and generally acting relieved that my defense had been a farce, a sham, a . . .

"Well, that went well, Janet."

Huh?

"Just like I told you when you first called me

about this, nobody wants to deal with a trial for such a small-potatoes case when the defendant is so blatantly guilty."

"Umm, Uncle Larry, what's the 'went well' part, exactly?"

"The 'went well' part is that now the judge will have a couple of free hours to catch up on paperwork this morning, so she'll be in a good mood for your sentencing."

"But what's my sentence going to be?"

"I told your mom this — didn't she fill you in? You've got no priors, you're a decent student, you play in the school jazz band, for Chrissakes. I think we're looking at a slap on the wrist for the criminal charges."

"And what about my license?"

"You'll probably get it a year or two late."

He clearly thought this was no big deal, and was kind of staring off distractedly over my shoulder at this point.

"A year or two late? All of my friends are going to have their licenses this year. I can't believe this.

Am I supposed to get a ride to the prom from my mother? How am I going to get to a summer job this year? This is so STUPID. I'm not a criminal. I didn't hurt anybody! I broke a lawn gnome. A LAWN GNOME!!! Isn't the judge going to see I'm harmless? Why didn't you fight this?"

A voice hovered over my left ear, and I knew what my uncle had been looking at. "He probably thought you would prefer human-service time to jail time. And he knew how much I HATE drunk driving."

Boy, those judges take short breaks.

SOLOMON

You know, you walk into a nursing home, and there's a lot to contend with. First of all, you're hit with that smell — like somebody just cooked up a rotting turkey carcass marinated in Lysol. Then there's the color scheme, with its exciting variations that run the full spectrum from white to off-white to beige. And the PEOPLE! There are grumpy-looking charge nurses ordering everyone around, grim-faced orderlies wheeling patients to and fro in wheelchairs and gurneys, the occasional detached doctor striding through on an urgent mission, and of course the patients. Okay, my mom told me to call them "residents" but who's kidding who here? They're sick, right? Therefore, they're patients.

Residents, my butt.

Anyway, all I'm trying to establish is that as I walked into the Egbert P. Johnson Memorial Home for the Aged to start my sentence, I was in no giggling mood, and the atmosphere therein wasn't likely to cheer me up anytime soon. I marched up to the third-floor north nurses' station, where they must have been expecting me. Three women were sitting with their heads sort of gaggled together, and they hushed up with an almost audible snap when I came around the corner from the elevator lounge.

"Hi, my name is Alex Gregory, and I've been assigned to work with Mr. . . . umm . . . Solomon Lewis. Am I in the right place?"

One of the three, a heavyset middle-aged woman whose name tag read CLAUDELLE GREEN, RN, looked me up and down, chuckled, and said, "Oh, you're in the right place, baby. We got the one and ONLY Solomon Lewis, don't we, girls?"

"Mmmmm, hmmmm," added a Miss Juanita Case, LPN, who was much younger, very pretty, and basically snickering in my face. "Your mother sure picked you a good one! Ever since we got our Solomon Lewis the other floors are all envious. Nobody else got anything LIKE a Solomon Lewis. Are you the new volunteer who's going to make Mr. Lewis all happy and cheerful for us?"

The third member of the trio was Leonora McCarthy, Certified Social Worker, a tiny woman who looked practically old enough to just get out of her chair and into a bed in one of the rooms. She said under her breath, "This ought to be a hoot." Then she looked at me and pointed to the first door on my right. "We keep Mr. Lewis in three-forty-four, so he's close to the station here and we can minimize the damage he does, so to speak. You can go in now; he loves getting a new volunteer. In fact, he's had about four different ones since July. Just one piece of advice: Don't be nice to him. He'll eat you up if you let him get an edge."

The other two echoed her with cries of "You got THAT right" and "You think this one will last through supper?"

You can imagine how delighted I was as I stepped into Room 344.

The room was standard hospital issue: white

walls, off-white floor tiles, turkey/Lysol scent. It had no decorations whatsoever — no cards, no "Get Well Soon" balloons, no family pictures. So the only thing I could possibly look at was the man on the bed. He was sitting, propped up on two pillows, staring at the TV with the sound off as he switched channels at lightning speed. His hair was a metallic gray, and his face was surprisingly red, which served to highlight his large, hooked peninsula of a nose. We once learned about Charles Darwin in ninth-grade biology class, and how he found something like thirteen different species of these birds called finches in the Galápagos Islands. I remember each species had a radically different beak shape. One kind used their beaks to make holes in trees. Then they would reach down into the openings at a steep angle and pull out grubs to eat. Well, Mr. Solomon Lewis would have fit in perfectly with those particular finches. Behind the beak, shadowed by his looming single eyebrow, two laser-blue eyes were doing their best to burn a hole in the TV screen. Beneath the beak was a regular, thin-lipped old-man mouth, drawn into the fiercest grimace I'd ever seen.

The overall effect: Solomon Lewis was an ancient, merciless gargoyle, armed with a remote control and a trigger-quick thumb.

I stood there in the doorway for a few minutes, semi-scared to speak. I cleared my throat softly, then more loudly. He had to know I was there, but was clearly dishing out the Silent Treatment. Well, Leonora McCarthy had warned me not to be nice, and I wasn't necessarily getting all huggy and teary-eyed watching this hawk-man ignore me, so I sat down in the big armchair next to his bed and waited. And waited. And waited. The only sound in the room was the buzz of the overhead lights, and the rattling wheeze of the old man's breathing. He was a remarkably loud breather.

After a few minutes of staring at his face and hoping he would give in and look at me, I tried tuning into the TV. Which had its own frustrations, because at the exact moment I became interested in any given channel, Solomon Lewis hit the clicker. It was uncanny. For the first but definitely not the last time I almost suspected the old man was reading my mind — like he had the superpower of dialing into the annoyance center of my brain.

When I had just about decided to jump up, block the screen, and burst into a few verses of "Getting to Know You," Solomon Lewis spoke.

"Sit up in that chair, you little *pisher*. Didn't anyone ever teach you about posture?"

"Excuse me, sir?"

"What are you, another slow kid? My last volunteer was such a *schmendrick*, he needed Velcro shirts because he couldn't do buttons. I said you should sit up."

All right, I had known I wouldn't be walking into a picnic here. But between this guy's tone and the unfamiliar foreign words he was throwing in, I was too stunned and confused to speak.

So he did the slow-talking thing that you might use for, like, a brain-damaged pet monkey. "Ssss-iiii-tttt uuuu-ppppp. Good boy. Maybe soon you can learn to stand up or even chew food. In the meantime, why are you here irritating defenseless old men when you should be in school, learning to hold a pencil or something?"

"Umm, Mr. Lewis, my name is Alex Gregory. I'm a high school student, and I'll be spending about ten hours here with you every week until . . . well, for a while."

"So, Alex, they send me here to be nursed, and you they send here to keep me out of the nurses' hair. Do you know what my grandmother would have said about this *cockamamie* situation?"

"I, uh, don't think so, sir."

"Well, I don't know either. *She's* dead, and *I'm* so forgetful that last week I tried to unlock my room door with my toothbrush. But she would have said something. God, that woman could talk! Once, when we were leaving Poland to come to America, I remember she spent so long *kibitzing* with the ticket taker that we almost missed the ship. Finally my grandfather says to her, 'Sadie, when we get to America, you can't be holding up people's business all the time with your *kibitzing.*' She says, 'Irv, when we get to America I won't say a thing.' He winks at me and says, 'Hallelujah, America really IS a new world!'"

I almost laughed out loud, but the moment was lost when another "resident" walked past the doorway behind me. Sol got out of bed, darted over to the door, and said, "Good afternoon, Mrs. Goldfarb."

Mrs. Goldfarb looked kind of startled and nervous when she saw who was addressing her. She gave a pinched little smile and murmured, "Hi, Sol. How are you today?"

"Fine, fine. But how many times have I told you that you have to put your TEETH in before you leave your room?"

She clamped her hand over her mouth, wheeled on her heels, and scurried back the way she'd come. "Gotcha!" Sol exclaimed with deep satisfaction. "That's the fourth time this week."

I was a bit slow to process this. "Umm, Mr. Lewis, her teeth WERE in."

"A rocket scientist, you aren't. Of course her teeth were in."

"But why did you —"

"Alex, *boychik*, if you're going to last at all in this crazy house, there's one thing you need to understand about the old people in here: They need to be kept on their toes. The minute you let them stop thinking, you might as well just put laughing gas in their oxygen tanks, crank it up, and finish 'em off."

I didn't have the slightest clue of how to respond to that, so I sat there shifting my weight from foot to foot, studying the stubborn Ring Ding stains on my sneakers. Solomon Lewis strode past me, chuckling to himself between loud breaths, and sat down on his bed. All of a sudden the chuckles were gone, and he was making this horrible "Hoo-hah-hoo-hah" noise. His hands were on his knees, and his head was hunched to his chest. I asked twice whether he needed help, but he didn't respond. The third time, I jumped up, went over, knelt down right in front of his face, and spoke loudly: "Mr. Lewis, are you okay?"

He glanced up with a mixture of anger and fear that I'd never seen on anybody before. "Don't — hoo-hah — worry. This is just what — hoo-hah — happens when I'm dying — hoo-hah — you imbecile!"

October 27

Dear Judge Trent,

I am writing to update you on my progress with the human-service project you assigned me. I think it is great that you gave me a chance to right my wrongs and learn from my mistakes, even though my accident did not hurt anybody but myself. However, I have just completed my first visit to the nursing home, where I worked with a very interesting ~~patient~~ resident named Solomon Lewis, and I feel you should change my assignment.

First of all, while I know the assignment is to serve humans, I am just not qualified to assist Mr. Lewis. Apparently, he has some problems with memory and attention that should be handled by a competent mental-health professional, rather than a teenager. He is also, frankly, verbally abusive. Within minutes of meeting me, Mr. Lewis called me an imbecile, said I was "not a rocket scientist" and "irritating," and suggested that maybe the other pati residents should be mercy-killed. He also berated me repeatedly in some foreign language, which the nurses said must be something called "Yiddish."

Secondly, nobody alerted me to this ahead of time, but Mr. Lewis is afflicted with a serious health problem called "emphysema." He started choking to death right in front of me, and I didn't have the skills to help him. A nurse had to come rushing in with a big mask and give him some kind of emergency breathing treatment. He survived, but it looked like a close call to me. Then when he finally caught his breath, I asked him whether he was feeling better, and he told me to, "Gay kocken offen yom!" I looked on the Internet when I got home, and apparently Mr. Lewis feels that, rather than assisting him at the nursing home, I should "Go take a dump in the ocean" instead.

In closing, I feel that I have grounds for concern

here. I am glad to do human service so that I can learn a valuable life lesson about responsibility and trust. However, I am just not qualified to meet Mr. Lewis's needs. The home should replace me with a psychiatrist/linguist/paramedic/saint, and the court should find me a new assignment that will be less traumatic for my sensitive adolescent mind.

Sincerely,

Alex Gregory

October 29

Dear Alex,

Contrary to your assertions, Mr. Lewis sounds like the perfect match for you.

As I explained to you when we accepted you into the Full Circle pretrial intervention pilot program, the human-service component is only half of the picture. The point of the program is that by working through the challenges and difficulties of serving others, you will ultimately be serving yourself. I look forward to more letters from you so that I can enjoy the unfolding process of your personal growth, and Mr. Lewis's, as well. In the meantime, you are hereby ordered to continue your service with Mr. Lewis.

Sincerely,

Judge J. Trent

P.S. A Yiddish phrase that might come in handy for your use with Mr. Lewis is "Bluz in toches!" Like Mr. Lewis, I am Jewish, and in the proud language of our people, this means "Blow it out your butt."

PLAN B

For my second visit to see Solomon Lewis, I had to pump myself up just to make it through the door. All the way on the bus to the home, my inner drill sergeant was delivering a high-energy sermon to my inner coward — who is remarkably similar to my outer coward, now that I think about it.

> **Drill Sergeant:** Buck up now, son. There's a job waitin' for you up in that room. Now you're just going to get in there and . . . and . . . and . . . HUMAN SERVE until I tell you to stop . . . uh . . . human servicin'!
>
> **Inner Coward:** But, sir, I'm not trained for this mission.
>
> **Drill Sergeant:** First, don't call me "sir." I *work* for a living. Second, you have all the training you need, boy. Now show some old-fashioned red-blooded American guts and GET IN THERE.

Inner Coward: Why should I?

Drill Sergeant: Why? WHY? There ain't no "why" in this man's army, son. You are just a weapon. The orders come down, and you attack. Does a *gun* ask why? Does a *tank* ask why?

Inner Coward: No, but what about a smart bomb? Does a smart bomb ask why?

Drill Sergeant: Umm ... uhh ... I'm not too sure about that technical stuff. I mean, I suppose you could *program* a smart bomb to ask why. But could it ask WHY it asked why? I guess the true question is whether a smart bomb can ever attain true awareness. In the immortal words of Socrates ...

Inner Coward: You're scaring me, sir.

Drill Sergeant: Doesn't matter. We've reached the drop zone. Now go, go, GO. And STOP CALLING ME "SIR"! I don't know why we let snot-nosed punks like you into the military anyway. When John Wayne was alive, you didn't see a bunch of lily-livered, weak-kneed, sniveling, scrawny pantywaists tryin' to make excuses for every . . .

Inner Coward: Thank you, Sergeant. You're an inspiration. Honestly.

I paused before entering Mr. Lewis's room, took a deep breath, and marched myself right in. The old man was sitting up in bed reading a book I had read in school, *Angela's Ashes*, by Frank McCourt. So I cleared my throat and tried to start right in with a discussion.

"Good morning, Mr. Lewis. I'm Alex, your volunteer. Remember?"

He just stared at me like I was a walking, talking fungus.

"Anyway, I read that book last year. Great, isn't it?"

"Who the hell are you? I've never seen you before in my life. Nurse. NURSE! Help! There's a thief in my room. I think he wants to —"

This was alarming. "Mr. Lewis, wait! I'm just your . . . um . . . I'm Alex."

"Help! Alex, the Um, is here to get me. NURSE!"

Claudelle came pounding through the doorway. "Mr. Lewis, calm down. It's okay." She gestured to me. "This is just . . ."

"Alex, the Um." Then Mr. Lewis started laughing so hard I thought he might start choking again. "Gotcha! Alex, the Um! Boy, are you two gullible."

Come to think of it, I kinda *hoped* he'd start choking again.

"So, Mr. Um, you liked *Angela's Ashes?*"

Maybe I could show him I wasn't so stupid. "Yes, I enjoyed the way he made his memoir feel like fiction."

"Oh, what a load of *chazzerai* that is. 'Made his memoir feel like fiction.' Ha! Did you like it? Did you cry? This book, do you know where it hit me? Right in the *kishkes*, it hit me. Pow! Those Irish, they know from suffering, let me tell you."

"Well, I *said* I liked it. It was deep."

"Deep, schmeep! Nurse, are you hearing Mr. Um here? For this, you're paying school taxes?"

Claudelle shook her head and clicked her tongue

as she walked away, leaving me to sink or swim in this riptide of undeserved criticism.

"Listen, Mr. Lewis, I don't know why you're picking on me. You liked the book, right? I liked the book. You liked it, I liked it — so don't torture me, okay?"

Mr. Lewis looked fairly pleased with me all of a sudden. "Call me Sol, Mr. Um. Now that you've raised your voice to me in anger, I figure we're on a first-name basis."

"I'm sorry, Mr. Lewis. I just didn't come here to get . . ."

"Listen, Mr. Um. First of all, I told you to call me Sol. Second of all, don't apologize for showing some backbone. Especially for a slow kid like you — no offense — you're going to need some of that *chutzpah* to get you through life. Everybody needs a meal ticket, and if you aren't blessed with looks or brains, a big mouth isn't such a bad substitute."

Wow, that was the most backhanded compliment I ever heard. But at least I've got *chutzpah*, whatever that is.

"Anyway, Mr. Um, what are we going to do today? We've already had our literature lesson for the week, so what do you think? Some chess, maybe? Or for you, checkers? Tic-tac-toe? Go fish? War?"

I don't know what on earth possessed me, but Sol had pressed my buttons again. "Hey, Sol, I've got about three more hours here tonight. How's about a nice friendly game of poker?"

Sol produced a pack of cards from his nightstand, and a bone-chilling grin spread across his face.

November 10

Dear Judge Trent,

As you know, when you stipulated as a condition of my probation that the nursing home assign me a "challenging" resident, my mother deliberately selected Mr. Lewis as the perfect match. I also know that, in your last letter, you supported my mother's selection. However, because my mother has a direct personal and financial stake in my case — one might even call it a "grudge" — I must once more implore you to reassign me.

Because I am a good and conscientious worker, I showed up for my fourth through sixth hours of service to Mr. Lewis on Thursday, November 9. However, as you will read below, things did not run smoothly. If the terms of successful completion for the Full Circle project are that I: a) teach someone a life lesson, b) learn a life lesson, and c) pay back the $500.00 in damages I did to Mrs. Wilson's lawn, accepting as I must her inflated claim that her little elf statuette was worth $374.59, I don't know how my time with Mr. Lewis will ever result in my release.

Number one, I don't know how I am going to teach Mr. Lewis anything. I tried to engage him in an intellectual discussion of literature on Thursday, but he was markedly unreceptive. He thinks I am stupid and funny-looking, so I don't think he is ready to believe I can offer him any wisdom at all. I told him at one point, "If you would listen to me for a minute, maybe I could teach you something." He replied, "And if my grandmother would grow wheels, maybe she'd be a trolley car."

Number two, Mr. Lewis cannot teach me

anything because he is too busy abusing me. I will admit I am picking up some choice Yiddish sayings. For example, I now know that a "schlemiel" is a clumsy man, and a "schlemazzel" is the schlemiel's victim. However, I would hate to believe that Mr. Lewis spilled a large glass of ice water in my lap for the sole purpose of improving my vocabulary. Also, vocabulary is not a life lesson. I might not be a rocket scientist. I might even be an imbecile or a schlemazzel. But I think I would know it if Mr. Lewis were able to enhance my personal growth, which is clearly not the case.

Number three, I know I am supposed to earn back the $500 for the garden sprite at $5.00 per hour. However, Mr. Lewis took advantage of my youth and innocence to swindle me out of $27.25 in a poker game. If I keep earning $15 a visit, and losing $27 and change, I will still be working here when it is time for them to move me into my own retirement room. That Mr. Lewis has a lot of chutzpah ripping off a defenseless teenager like that!

Please let me offer you a final assurance that I

am not lazy. I would gladly build houses for Habitat for Humanity, or carry fifty-pound water jugs for the Special Olympics. I'd cheerfully and eagerly paint playgrounds, spackle schools, dig ditches. I will shovel out stables, mow the grass of every park in town. I'd be thrilled to wash the whole fleet of police cars by hand — which would also be a more fitting punishment for my particular "crime." If you spare me the torment of another ninety-four hours of Solomon Lewis, I will do your bidding for TWO hundred hours ANYWHERE, ANYTIME.

Just say the word and I will put on my work gloves.

Sincerely,

Alex Gregory

Your Damp and Frozen Schlemazzel

November 14

Dear Alex,

    Keep plugging away there. I think you are on the verge of a marvelous breakthrough.

Sincerely,

Judge J. Trent

P.S. — "Schlemazzel" is not such a horrible insult. If Mr. Lewis starts calling you a "meshuggener," or "crazy man," that's when you will know you are being insulted.

LAURIE MEETS SOL

"**So,** Laurie, Princess, is your husband here a *meshuggener*, or what?"

"Mr. Lewis, Alex is *not* my husband. We're only sixteen years old. Besides, I told you, he's my best friend. He has no romantic interest in me at all."

"I know. That's why he's a *meshuggener!*"

• • •

There are certain things on earth that just don't mix. Oil and water come to mind. Cobras and mongooses. Lit cigarettes and barrels of dynamite.

Alcohol and lawn gnomes.

But if there was ever a combination that filled my heart with terror and dread, that recipe for disaster was Laurie and Sol.

Of course, I was still best friends with Laurie. Ever since my hearing, she had stopped bugging me about the accident. At first she had been trying to show sympathy because of the whole driver's license thing. Now, she was just too busy enjoying my tales of misery. Every Wednesday and Friday in home-room, she would dash up to me with a barely hidden grin and ask, "How was your visit with Sol last night?"

So I'd tell her the highlights: He suckered me in poker and froze my leg. Or he called me a chimp. Or he hid Mrs. Goldfarb's wig in the planter again.

Laurie's eyes would sparkle with demented pixie dust as she said, "So when can I meet this guy?"

What was a boy to do? For someone who always scolded me about my bad ideas, she sure was blind to her own disaster potential. Can you imagine what he'd say to her? What she'd say to him? What they would *do* to each other?

I had visions of epic battles with remote con-trols, wheelchairs, Chinese throwing stars pinging off the old man's oxygen tank. But somehow it never crossed my mind that the irresistible force and the immovable object would become fast friends.

So here we were at the historic first meeting. Maybe I should hit the rewind button so you can catch the whole painful encounter.

It was a Friday night, and Laurie stopped by my house. Mom was walking in frantic little circles in the kitchen, getting ready for her second big first date — the original "Mister Right" hadn't wanted to see her again after my little vehicular adventure interrupted their evening. Mom was afraid I'd do something stupid while she was out, and Laurie saw her chance to strike.

"Mrs. Gregory, I have the perfect way to keep Alex out of trouble."

"So do I, but the child welfare people think it's cruel and unusual to cage him up with the dog again." That mom of mine and her wacky child-abuse humor!

"This might be less satisfying for you, but it's totally legal. Wanna hear it?"

"Laurie, sweetheart, could you get my top button in the back there? Okay, what's the plan?"

"I'll take custody of the boy, and bring him on the bus to the nursing home to visit Mr. Lewis." Ignoring my gasp, my dirty look, and my vicious ankle kick, she continued with her charming-the-parents voice. "We'll kill three birds with one stone: You will be free for the evening and Alex won't have access to a car, Alex will get in some extra hours with Mr. Lewis and impress the probation people, and I won't have to sit home all alone because my loser best friend is grounded."

"Hmm . . . let me think for a minute. Is this necklace too clunky for the dress?"

"No, it's nice. So what do you think of the plan?"

"Sorry, honey, but Alex is staying put."

I smiled, and it was Laurie's turn to kick MY ankle. "Mrs. Gregory, why don't you wear the little gold hoop earrings? They really set off your eyes."

"I already said no, dear." My mom picked up her tiny, fancy-looking purse-thingie.

"I know. I just think you should be well accessorized for your big night. You have your cell phone, right?"

"Yes, but why? Alex knows where I'll be: at the Pluto Grill, on the river."

Laurie gave me her sweetest and most sinister smile. "Alex knows where you'll be, but the police and ambulance crews don't."

Just then a car horn beeped outside. My mom looked at Laurie. Laurie grinned at my mom. Mom snarled. "Oh, take him, you rotten thing. But you *will* have him home by the time I get back." Then she realized this had come out sounding a tad harsh, so she gave Laurie a quick hug and muttered, "Take care of him for me, okay?"

Mom dashed out the door before I could mention my own vast, legendary ability to take care of myself. Laurie turned to me and said, "Grab your coat. And don't get too carried away thanking me — you'll make me blush!"

I was too mad to say much on the bus ride, but as we got off the bus and started walking into the home, I couldn't let Laurie go in there without a warning. Even the Queen of Manipulation deserved some preparation before she headed into battle. So I gave her all of the tips I'd picked up: Go easy on the eye contact, never show friendliness, don't go out on a limb with personal information, opinions, or observations. She wanted to know what she COULD do. "Run away home, child," was all I could come up with.

Nurse Claudelle came around the corner as we were emerging from the elevator, overheard the end of my speech, and clucked her tongue at me. "Why are you telling tales on our Mr. Lewis? Don't listen to this one, honey. Solomon Lewis is a fine old gentleman. By the way, Alex, where have you been hiding this sweet little thing? Hi, my name is Claudelle Green. I'm the charge nurse on the unit here. You must be very proud of Alex. We got him all worried about Mr. Lewis before his first visit, but he marched in there like a trooper and things have been going fine ever since. Isn't that right, Alex?"

I spluttered. "He — you — you all said he was — Wait! She's not a sweet little thing. She's my friend Laurie."

Claudelle clucked again. "Miss Laurie, you've got a nice boy here. IF he ever learns some manners and starts telling you that you ARE a sweet little thing."

69

I stomped into Sol's room, just to get away from the baffling female madness. Sol was reading Hemingway this time, *The Old Man and the Sea*. He held the book up to me for comment, but before I could say anything, he started in: "Ah, Mr. Um. So nice to see you — and on a Friday, no less. Did you come by to give me an extra literature lesson? Some poker advice, maybe?"

Then he saw Laurie over my shoulder, and broke into a mammoth grin. It was like a friendly, body-snatching alien had abducted him and taken his place. I figured those thin little lips would snap under the unaccustomed tension, but they held. "Oh, and you brought a friend. Isn't that what the young men are calling their young ladies these days?"

Laurie beamed right back at him. Hadn't she listened to my advice AT ALL? "Hello, Mr. Lewis. My name is Laurie. I'm so glad to meet you. Alex talks about you all the time."

Good golly. This was turning into some sort of sickening love fest.

"About *me*, he talks? When he's looking into

those pretty eyes of yours, it's not about *me* your friend should be talking."

On second thought, at any moment Sol was probably going to trigger Laurie's fabled Anti-Sexist Death Stare, and then we'd all be diving for cover.

"Oh, stop it, Mr. Lewis. Alex and I are just best friends."

"With the way he's looking at you, I figure I should start calling him your husband."

"Friend, Mr. Lewis. F-r-i-e-n-d. Fffrrrriiiieeeennn-nnndddd."

"Husband. Laurie, darling, trust me. Husband."

"Friend, amigo, buddy. You know — like, pal? Friend."

"Husband."

"Friend."

Which is where we came in a few pages ago. I couldn't believe this. Laurie and Sol were bantering, or sparring, or flirting, or something. Not that I cared, aside from the creepiness. Since she and I were just friends, after all. And what did Sol mean, exactly, about the way I looked at her?

Wait. The guy was old, grumpy, and at least half insane. Why was I even thinking about this? I needed to clear my head.

"Sol, since you and my wife are hitting it off so well, I think I'll just go fill out my time forms at the nurses' station, okay?" He didn't even look away from Laurie, but kinda waved his hand at me in dismissal.

I walked out, trying to tune out the conspiratorial laughter behind me, and sat down behind the desk at the station. Claudelle was there, drinking coffee. She started talking with me about her kids, her husband's health problems, and her aching feet, and I listened for a good, long while — she was a pretty interesting lady when she wasn't teasing me. Plus, it was easier than trying to handle the two-headed runaway freight train of Sol and Laurie. But eventually Claudelle let out a huge sigh, and eased herself back onto her sore tootsies. If she was getting back into action, I supposed I should be, too.

Back in the room, the scene was a shocker. Sol was sitting in his chair, and Laurie was fluffing the pillows on his bed. "Laurie, honey pie, you might be prettier than Alex, but when he makes my bed, he does hospital corners. Floppy sheets is not my idea of comfortable. And this water, it's too warm. Alex always gets me ice from the fourth floor."

"But, Mr. Lewis, I don't usually do those . . ."

Laurie spun and cut me off. "You don't make his bed?"

"No, the nurses' aides do that."

"You don't fluff his pillows?"

"Nope."

"But you do go get him water, right?"

"Nuh-uh."

Laurie looked back and forth from me to Sol, whose facial expression was starting to look familiar. "So I'm guessing you never, um, rub his feet?"

Sol finally broke out with his booming bark: "Gotcha!"

I told her not to be nice to him, but apparently, wives never listen.

SOL GETS INTERESTED

The next week, I got to Sol's late because I had jazz band practice after school. We'd gotten this new chart called "Jumpin' with Symphony Sid," and I was struggling with it. The accents were all in really strange places, so I kept hitting the accented notes at the wrong time. Or I'd get the timing right, but concentrate so hard on THAT that I'd slip into the wrong key. Then the conductor, Mr. Watras, would stop the band and try to correct me, which was embarrassing. I never did get it right at the rehearsal, but Mr. Watras must have decided to just ignore my spastic rhythm and blatant pitch errors.

So anyhow, that's why I was late. And Sol wasn't in his room. At the nurses' station, Juanita Case was on duty. She seemed a little annoyed that she'd missed the big night with Laurie, which had provided endless hours of laughter for the staff when Sol had told them about it. Still, having missed the original action didn't disqualify her from picking on me about it.

"So how's the Pillow Fluff Girl? Will she be back soon? Sol's pillows are looking a mite droopy."

"Oh, please give me a break, Miss Case. I just spent an hour getting publicly humiliated in jazz band at school, and now I have to see Sol. I'm not sure how much more I can take in one day."

"How did they humiliate you up at that school?"

"Oh, it wasn't the school, it was me. I just couldn't get my parts right today."

"Well, baby, Sol is at hydrotherapy right now, and he won't be back for a good half hour. Why don't you close yourself up in his room and practice that guitar?"

So I did. I set up my music on the edge of the bed, sat in the chair with my Tele, and played through "Jumpin' with Symphony Sid" over and over. After about fifteen minutes, I was starting to get the rhythm and the notes right at the same time — as long as I didn't try to think about what I was doing.

The instant I started to think, I'd mess up again. My old middle school English teacher, Miss Palma, used to talk to my class about how we should be "Writing Zen Masters" who could "think without thinking." Weird, right? She always said writing was like bike riding, and that if you ever stopped and thought about HOW you were balancing on your bike, you'd fall. Even though I thought Miss Palma might have spent a little too much time on mountaintops, I never forgot the advice. So while I was playing this piece, I concentrated so hard on not concentrating that I didn't hear Sol being wheeled in behind me until he started whistling the melody of the song over the chords I was playing. I stopped and turned to say hi.

"So today you're serenading me, Mr. Um? To what do I owe this privilege? Is it maybe 'Sing to a Fossil Day'? And why is your music paper on my bed? I'm telling you, the service around here is slipping without that lovely Laurie girl here."

I jumped up, almost dropping the Tele in the

process, and grabbed up the sheet music with a fast sweep of my hand. "I'm sorry, Sol. I was just early for our visit, so I decided to use the time practicing."

"Wait a minute, Mr. Um. You weren't early, you were late. Just because I can't breathe doesn't mean I can't tell time. And what is that thing in your lap?"

"It's a guitar."

"This much, I know. I mean, what is it doing in your lap?"

"Well, I play it. I mean, I play in the school jazz band. I'm not very good, but I . . ."

Sol got out of the wheelchair and into bed. "You play fine. I knew what song it was, didn't I? Now, why don't you make yourself useful and play for me?"

"Well, I don't know many of this kind of songs. Plus, I don't even have my amplifier with me, so it's not going to be loud enough."

"So play what you know, as loud as you play. It has to be better than hearing your thoughts on Hemingway. I promise I won't criticize."

Well, that would be a refreshing change, anyway.

I took out the only other sheet music I had in my case, which was a Miles Davis tune from the 1960s called "All Blues." I carried it around and played it all the time because it was much easier than most of the jazz we played in school. I used to try to get Mr. Watras to call for it at every rehearsal so I could have three minutes of not feeling like a complete half-wit. I also just liked Miles Davis. I once read a book about him for a biography project at school — he was tough and confident, and used to play with his back to the audience sometimes because he didn't care what people thought. So of course they all flipped over him — women used to line up to meet him, and he was like a rock star before there even were rock stars. He was kind of like Laurie with a trumpet, in a lot of ways. Anyhow, I got the music arranged on the nightstand, counted it off to myself (1-2-3, 1-2-3), and started playing. I was nervous, so I started the song at a pretty quick tempo.

"Slower," Sol muttered. So I slowed down. I looked up about halfway through the chart, and his eyes were closed. His face looked almost peaceful, and his breathing was the quietest it had ever been in my presence. I figured I was either impressing him or putting him in a coma. For the last chorus, I played harder and more rhythmically, and Sol's fingers started rubbing together in the ghost of a snap. So he was dialed into what I was playing, which was both cool and scary.

When I stopped, and the last dominant-seventh chord was still floating in the air like a bell you might have once heard in a sad dream, Sol opened his eyes and looked at me. I couldn't read anything in his expression at all. Did he like the song? Did he think I'd played well? Was he really not going to criticize?

"More," he whispered hoarsely. "More."

I couldn't believe it. I had found something I could do that Solomon Lewis liked.

And, try as I might, I couldn't see a "Gotcha" angle anywhere.

November 22

Dear Judge Trent,

I am writing today with my first piece of positive news. As you may remember from my hearing, I play the guitar, and am a member of my high school's jazz band. This week, Mr. Lewis asked me to play my guitar for him, and I did. The playing seemed to entertain him. As I was leaving for the day, Mr. Lewis even told me, "If you ever want to practice more for somebody old and defenseless, feel free. I'm stuck here in bed anyway." Which is the kindest thing he has said to me yet.

I don't know how this will allow me to learn a lesson or teach one, but at least while I'm playing the guitar, Mr. Lewis is not mocking me, swindling me, or spilling icy beverages on my innocent flesh.

Thank you for your faith in me.

Sincerely,

Alex Gregory

HALF AN ANSWER

IN December, there was a serious cold snap. My mom finally un-grounded me so I could go shopping for her Christmas presents, but I spent tons of time in my basement practicing my jazz tunes for Sol. I even bought a tiny amplifier the size of a Walkman so I could play a little louder during my visits, even though the extra $30.00 added six hours to my sentence at the home. And twice a week, I dragged my Tele and the mini-amp onto the bus and up to Sol's room.

One day, I had just walked in when Sol asked me, "Where's your little wife, Laurie?"

"We're friends, Sol."

"About this, my grandmother had a saying: '*A halber entfer zogt oiget epes.*' That means, 'Half an answer also says something!'"

"Whatever. Do you want to hear something new I've been working on, just for you?"

"Oh, just for me, heh? Not for your tremendous worldwide audience, then?"

"Ha-ha. Do you want to hear it or not?"

"Who says I don't want to hear it? I'm sitting here, aren't I? You're a very sensitive boy, Alex. You have to toughen up, or the world will be a hard place for you."

"I'm not sensitive, Sol. You have no idea how strong I am."

"Oh, and *you* have an idea how strong you are? How do you know, with the easy life you kids are having nowadays? Strong, schmong!"

"Anyway, Sol, I'm going to play now." And I played a piece I had dug out of the jazz-band folder at school. I wanted to do something that Sol would know was just for him, so I found the medley from this play called *Fiddler on the Roof*. It's about a Jewish guy in the old country somewhere whose daughter wants to marry a guy who's not Jewish. I figured he would like to hear something a little different, and maybe he could relate to it or something. I had worked really hard on the piece, because the school's music was only for the piano, and it's hard to rewrite piano music for the guitar. Actually, it was probably the most effort I had put into anything since before my dad had moved out.

The medley starts out with this funny song called "Tradition." It's a big "oompah-oompah" kind of thing, and pretty fast. Then it segues into "Matchmaker, Matchmaker," which is the easiest part — a fast waltz with a simple melody. Next comes another "oom-pah" part called "To Life," which is the translation of a Jewish toast, *L'Chaim*. I was pretty proud that I knew that — Sol always said it right before he swallowed his pills. Anyway, the part after that is called "Sunrise, Sunset." It's a song the father sings about how he can't believe his daughter is old enough to move out and get married. It's a bittersweet kind of waltz and was really pretty when I didn't mess up the big finger stretches I had to pull off in order to play through its chord changes. Which was about forty percent of the time, but hey — I was tryin'.

So I started playing. You know how in, like, a Disney movie or something, the princess will start singing and all the birds and bees and deer and stuff will gather around to listen? This was a lot like that, but the birds, bees, and deer had walkers, wigs, and hearing aids. Residents came in. Nurses came in. Mrs. Goldfarb almost came in, but couldn't quite get herself to enter Sol's room, so she was just sort of leaning on the door frame.

"Tradition" flew by under my fingers. "Matchmaker, Matchmaker" might have been a tad slow, but when I looked over at Sol, he was nodding in time like he was conducting me with his fearsome eyebrow. "To Life" was great — I had the little Gypsy-sounding rhythm part really snapping along. And then I started to ease my way into "Sunrise, Sunset."

But as soon as I played maybe the fourth note of the first line ("Is this the little girl I carried?"), I chanced to look at Sol again, and what I saw made my fingers trip and crash all into one another, like the Three Stooges had suddenly taken possession of my digits. His head was bowed to his chest, and it looked as though he was crying silently. I stumbled through the rest of the song, and all of the assembled oldsters clapped, but by the end all I wanted was to find out what was wrong with Sol. As soon as the others started walking out, I turned to the bed.

"Sol, are you all right?"

No response.

"Sol? Mr. Lewis?"

He ignored me just long enough for the clacking of the last cane to fade off down the hallway, and then looked up. His eyes were still brimming and bloodshot. "I'm fine, Alex. What? A man can't be moved by some music once in a while?"

"But I didn't mean to make you upset. This was supposed to be, like, your Hanukkah present."

"Alex, Alex. I'm not upset. You gave me a very nice present. New socks, I don't need. A sweater from the mall, I don't want. Music, I like. And you played all right today."

"I did?"

"Don't fish for a compliment, *boychik* — it's not

dignified. I'm not saying you should quit your day job and head for Broadway, but you're learning something."

He watched without saying anything as I packed up my guitar, and I wondered why that one song would make him so emotional. I was feeling rather brave, since I had been such a big musical hit with him lately, so I asked. "Sol, was there something about that Sunrise song that bothered you?"

He smiled tightly, without showing a single tooth. "I didn't so much enjoy the part where you lost the time and played all the wrong notes. Other than that, I'm fine."

Right before he kicked me out of his room for the day, I told him a saying I'd just heard: "Half an answer also says something!"

HAPPY HOLIDAYS

Christmas break was looking grim. I planned to visit the old man every day of the vacation so I could really pack in the hours, but that wasn't exactly a one-way ticket to Party Land. Plus, Laurie was in New York with her mom until just before New Year's Eve, and my mom was working double shifts at the home so that "other people can enjoy time with their families."

What was I, her dog? Her goldfish, maybe? A really, really under-qualified chauffeur?

Of course, my mom wasn't my whole family. And the missing one-third of our little trio was sitting on Mom's front step one day when I got back from a day at the home.

Dad looked tired and kind of old. I stopped about ten feet in front of him, wondering how long he'd been sitting there in the freezing weather, with nothing but a suit jacket to keep him warm and his expensive wing-tip shoes frosted in the drifting snow. He's some kind of junior vice-president guy at the local bank, and is always dressed super-fancy, even hours after work. But for the first time I could ever remember, his face was completely covered in stubble.

"Hi, Alex."

"Uh, hi, Dad."

"It's been a while. You know, I called a few times."

"Yeah, I've been really busy with my community service, and school, and the SATs are coming up. I was going to call you, but — you know . . ."

"And I sent you some e-mails."

"Yeah, my stupid mail server has been acting up."

"Well, that would explain why you blocked all messages from my address, I suppose. What a relief. I thought you were mad at me." Boy, between Mom's sarcasm, and Dad's, Laurie's, and Sol's, it's a wonder I even stay sane. "Anyway, I just came by to see you before . . . before . . . well, I'm going out of town for a while."

"What do you mean, out of town?"

"I've accepted a job in Philadelphia. It starts on January fifteenth."

"But that's like an hour and a half away. It's in a whole 'nother state."

"I know. That's why it's considered 'out of town.'"

"Are you taking the home-wrecker with you?"

"You mean, Sandy?"

"Uh, yeah, Mrs. Simonsen, my third-grade teacher who made you break up with Mom."

"She didn't make — oh, whatever, Alex. Things aren't as simple as they appear to you. No, she isn't coming with me. We broke up a few weeks ago. That's one of the things I was calling to tell you."

"So why are you moving?"

"I need a change, Alex. I need to get away from all this." He made a sweeping gesture that took in everything around, including his only son.

"Well, thanks for telling me. I guess leaving Mom and me wasn't enough of a change, huh?"

"Look, Alex, I didn't come here to fight, but

you're just wrong about this. I didn't 'leave' your mother — she kicked me out. Like I said, things aren't so simple. People are complicated and contrary."

"Mom kicked *you* out? I don't believe it."

"Well, I don't want to say anything bad about your mother, but she did."

"Why?"

"That's not important, Alex. What's important is that I'm trying to be your father, and you aren't letting me."

"You're trying to be my father by moving out of state? Wow, thanks for the show of support."

"It's not like that, Alex. Look — do you remember when Wink died?"

Wink was our cat when I was five. He ran out in front of a car because I had left the front door open and he'd gotten out. My parents had hidden the truth from me for weeks. "Yeah, are you trying to tell me he really just moved to Philadelphia?"

Dad nearly smiled, and he suddenly looked a lot like my old dad, my Little League-coaching, arm-wrestling-before-bed, taking-long-walks-to-see-the-turtles-in-the-park dad. "No, I'm saying sometimes parents try to shield their kids from hard facts. Maybe one day, Mom will be willing to tell you why she told me to leave. But that's between you and her."

Mom's car turned the corner at the head of our block, and my dad jumped up from the snowy stoop. "Gotta go, kid. Are we friends?"

"I don't know, Dad. I'll call you. Does your phone still work?"

"My cell does."

He struggled a bit with his frozen hands and his ice-cold car keys, but still managed to get the door of his fast little midlife-crisis mobile open before Mom could pull up and start arguing. He ruffled my hair, which he hadn't done since maybe sixth grade, hopped in the car, and zoomed off.

If he had told me the truth about the divorce, then he wasn't the bad guy. So who was?

Mom walked over to me. "What was that about?"

"Philadelphia, Mom."

"Philadelphia, the city?"

"No, Philadelphia, the cream cheese."

Tough family.

• • •

The next time I went to Sol's, it was three days after Christmas, and also the first night of Hanukkah. I hadn't prepared another special song or anything, so I stopped and bought Sol a book about jazz history. He was sitting in his chair staring at a huge vase of white flowers on his nightstand. The vase had a blue-and-white bow around it. Sol had a transparent tube wrapped around his head and stuck right under his nose. The tube made a constant hissing noise, so he didn't hear me until I was right in front of him. He looked groggy, and only gave me a little nod. Even that looked like a big effort.

What the heck? I decided he'd explain if he wanted to, and that I'd pretend everything was normal.

"Sol, how are you? Happy Hanukkah."

He muttered, "Happy Hanukkah. Where's — HOO-hah — your guitar?"

"I didn't bring it today, but I got you a book about jazz. It's called *Monk*, and it's about this great, crazy piano player named Thelonious Monk. Have you ever heard of him?"

The next thing Sol said sounded a lot like, "I knew him."

But of course it was hard to make out the exact words, and I didn't want to make Sol talk more than he had to, so I just nodded. "Nice flowers. Who brought them?" It had never occurred to me that Sol might have other visitors.

"I did. Claudelle went . . . to the . . . store with me. On . . . her day off. For my . . . daughter . . . Judy. HOO-hah! She's a hotshot lawyer. Very smart. Very . . . busy."

"They're beautiful. I'm sure she'll love them."

"Yeah. Heh. She . . . always liked . . . flowers. Her mother, too — always with the flowers. HOO-hah. 'Sol, did you get me any flowers? Sol, let's plant . . . a garden. Sol, those are GORGEOUS! A little past their — HOO-hah — prime, maybe, but — nice.'"

He took a few moments to catch his breath and let go of his memories, and I spoke over his gasps. "Are you comfortable? Can I get you anything?"

"Does this, to you, look so comfortable? HOO-hah!"

"Well, I mean . . . what happened?"

"Nothing. I was walking . . . in the store with . . . Claudelle. Such a heart, that girl has. Like gold. Anyway . . . I walked too far. So now . . . I need . . . a little breathing help. That's all."

"Can they do anything to make it better?"

"Well, they're giving me . . ." He touched the tube around his face. "Oxygen. And breathing treatments. And some pills, I don't know. HOO-hah."

"Is it working?"

"If I'm not dead, it's working. If I die, you'll — HOO-hah — know it wasn't maybe working so good."

I had never asked him about his health before, but now seemed like as good a time as any. "They told me when I started here that you have emphysema. How long have you had it?"

"A million years. I don't know . . . *boychik.* Too . . . long."

"How did you get it?"

"It's funny, Alex. You smoke a million, two million — HOO-hah — cigarettes, and they don't . . . hurt you. But you take one . . . puff . . . of number two million and one — and all of a sudden you're — HOO-HOO-hah — in the hospital. Do you smoke?"

"No."

"Good. Don't start, or I'll have to get up and give you . . . a *klop* on the *tuchis*."

He looked up at me, and his eyes were more tired than I'd ever thought eyes could be. "Lesson over. Class — HOO-hah — dismissed. Now get out of here and let . . . an old man . . . read in peace."

I stopped at the nurses' station, where Claudelle was talking with Leonora. "She never comes. We buy her them *damn* flowers every year, but she never comes. And now her daddy's all wired up in there."

"I heard the paramedics almost had to intubate him."

"Forget that. They almost had to shock him, right in the middle of aisle five of Kmart. It was like he was the Blue Code Special. But he got his flowers for Judy, the Big-Shot Lawyer."

"A shame. He's really almost a sweet man, sometimes."

"You got it a little mixed up, Leo. Sometimes he's sweet and sometimes he's almost a man!"

They both laughed a little, and then their voices subsided as they turned their attention to me. Claudelle spoke. "How are you today, Alex?"

"Is he going to die?"

"Not today, child. Not today. He's a tough old thing, don't you worry. You'll get in your hundred hours before this is all over."

This made me mad. "That's NOT why I asked."

"I'm sorry, baby. I know that. Sol will be all right in a day or two, long as he doesn't get the pneumonia again, like Mrs. Johnson last spring."

"Who's Mrs. Johnson? I don't think I've seen her around."

Both women just looked at me blankly, until I realized I wasn't EVER going to see Mrs. Johnson around. I had to get out of there. I mumbled something about having to catch my bus, and headed for the elevator like I was getting off a sinking ship, at least for a couple of days. Not that I had been keeping count, no matter what Claudelle had said, but I still had forty-four hours left with Mr. Lewis.

December 27

Dear Judge Trent,

I am just checking in with my December update. It was a hard month, but I think I may have learned a lesson: You can't just throw somebody out of your life when they displease you. Mr. Lewis has this daughter somewhere who's a lawyer, and every year he buys her flowers for Hanukkah. He puts them on his nightstand, and then he waits and waits for the daughter to show up and get them. But she never does. Maybe he's so grouchy because his daughter doesn't love him. I'm getting used to his grumpiness, though. He threatened today to give me a klop on the tuchis, which I looked up and learned is a smack on the butt. However, he actually said it kind of affectionately.

I know I am halfway done with my mandated hundred hours of community service, and just a few weeks ago I was counting the days with glee. However, am I allowed to keep this job past the 100 hours if I wish to do so? It just seems that Mr. Lewis could use the company more than I could use the free time, especially since I can't drive and my family is falling apart anyway.

Sincerely,

Alex Gregory

THE BALL FALLS

ON New Year's Eve day, I messed some things up. I don't know why, because I woke up in a fine mood. My plan for the day was to practice guitar for a couple of hours, and then maybe go over to see Sol after lunch. My mom had a date that night (which made two nights in a row), and Laurie was going to come over and have a little loser-geek slumber party with me. When I got to the kitchen, I made a big pot of coffee and got out Mom's favorite mug, which for some reason featured my first-grade Mother's Day drawing of three Ninja Turtles under a tree with a huge machine gun. When I was little, I used to make coffee for both of my parents and serve it to them in bed sometimes. They would sit up and I would climb between them with my own special "coffee" drink, which was really just nuked milk with sugar in it. There were days we sat there snuggled up, playing little tickle games and laughing for hours, or at least it seemed like that to me. And no matter how hot my feet got under the covers with my footie pj's on, I never, ever wanted to be the first one to leave the bed. Interestingly enough, that honor generally fell to my dad.

Okay, enough of my sob stories. The thing was, I had the feeling my mom's date the night before hadn't been so ultra-groovy, because she had marched in at maybe nine P.M. without saying a word to me and stomped off to bed. So I made her the pot of coffee for old times' sake, or to cheer her up, or possibly just because I am just a much more swell son than you may have gathered thus far. When she came down, the obvious depressed-mom danger signs were there: the puffy eyes, the ancient terry-cloth bathrobe, even the dreaded hair curlers. This was a woman who probably needed to skip the caffeine and go right into electroshock therapy.

But since I didn't have the right equipment for home mom-zapping, I filled the mug and held it out to her. She said, "Do I look that bad?"

"No, Mom. I just had the coffee all made anyway, so I figured you could put your feet up, relax, and enjoy a cup. Why would you look bad?"

"Oh, nothing. I'll be fine."

Not "I'm fine," I noticed. "I'll BE fine," which is different.

"Do you want to talk?"

She looked at me and snapped, "What, should I be getting my life advice from you, of all people?"

Holy crap. That was basically uncalled for.

"Ho-kay, Mom. I'm going out now. Have a nice day and a happy new year!"

She may have been shouting, "Wait," and trying to apologize as I left the house, but with my Walkman on and blasting, I just saw a weird scary lady in a bathrobe standing on our porch with her arms waving.

My next stop was the home. I was starving, so I picked up some candy and a pack of cookies from a vending machine in the lobby, and gulped most of it down in the elevator. When I walked into Sol's room, he looked a lot better. His oxygen-tube thing was gone, and he was pacing back and forth. The white flowers were gone, too.

"Good afternoon, Mr. Um," he said almost cheerfully. "How are you today? I liked the book you gave me, even though Monk was a more interesting man in person."

I had to ask. "You met Thelonius Monk?"

"Many times. What, you think I was born here? I had a very interesting life in the old days."

"I'm sure you did."

"Anyway, how were your holidays, Alex?"

At that moment I could have tried to stop Sol from changing the subject, but I just didn't feel like risking an argument. Naturally, I got one anyway. AND I missed some info that could have changed everything.

"Fine." We were both big communicators today.

"'Fine,' he says. What 'fine?' How are things? Did you get nice presents? How are your parents? How is the little wife? I hope you're taking her somewhere special tonight. Hey, maybe you could drop by here with her on your way to do your young people monkey business."

Young people monkey business?

"Sol, we're just staying in tonight, at my house, if you really want to know."

"Without a chaperone? Better you should come here. We'll get some cups and some drinks, and I'll keep the two of you from doing anything you might regret."

"Sol, nothing is going to happen between us. We're just friends. My mom trusts us, so why can't you?"

"Sure she trusts you. She isn't a man. She doesn't know how you think. I remember how it is to be with a beautiful girl . . . alone . . . in the moonlight. But do what you think is best."

"Okay, I get the point, Sol. I'm a deranged, hormonal fiend, and no female is safe anywhere near me, even if she's a deadly martial-arts expert AND we're just friends. So, you want us to come here tonight?"

"*Boychik*," he said, reaching over to grab a pack of licorice out of my hand, "I thought you'd never ask!"

Wow, I had spoken to only two people the whole day: one who bit my head off for getting her some coffee, and one who manipulated me into spending my New Year's Eve at the old folks' home. The thought occurred to me that maybe life would be better if I had been born without a tongue.

Especially now that I had to tell Laurie I'd booked us an extra-wild party night.

I took the bus over to Laurie's house, where she was sitting in her kitchen, in her bathrobe, with a coffee mug. I almost turned and ran when I saw the déjà vu scene, but then — unlike my mom — she looked happy to see me. I had the horrible thought all of a sudden that she really WAS very pretty. When she hugged me, it was like Sol had put an evil spell on me: The Curse of Noticing Laurie. I somehow managed to push the thought away as we got ourselves arranged at the table, and soon I launched into a recap of the week's torments. It turned out, though, that Laurie hadn't had the peachiest time in New York.

"My dad is nuts."

"No, MY dad is nuts."

"Well, my MOM is nuts."

"So's mine."

"Oh, yeah? I bet YOUR dad isn't fleeing to another state to get away from YOU, Laurie."

"I bet YOUR dad isn't accusing you of treason for wanting to spend a few days with your mom, Alex."

"Well, that's just because my dad doesn't WANT me."

"Well, my mom doesn't want me, but I just went and spent Christmas with her. And she got me a swell present." Laurie started to cry, which is pretty rare for her.

"What?"

"She's pregnant."

"Wait, isn't she, like, too old?"

"Apparently, some random guy she met online didn't think so."

And the grown-ups don't think WE can be trusted together.

Somehow, Laurie and I wound up hugging each other for a bit too long then, until suddenly we both jumped up and away. Laurie fled to the upstairs bathroom to take a shower, and I went to the couch, watched MTV, and tried not to dwell on the scent of her hair. Holding her had felt so right, and so wrong, that I knew it was going to be a long evening. Which reminded me: I hadn't told Laurie about the groovy new plan for our intergenerational New Year's festivities. Fortunately, when she came back down and I laid the news on her, she took it well. Or at least she only hit me twice and called me "The Nerd King."

After a couple of hours shopping for snacks to bring to the oldsters, Laurie and I stopped at my house to drop off her overnight bag. I didn't feel like facing my mom, but it turned out she wasn't home anyway. There was a note on the table:

Hi, Honey. I am sorry to have snapped at you. I was upset, as you may have noticed, but everything will be fine. Also, I meant to tell you that Judge Trent called me. She's so impressed with your progress that she said you don't need to see a probation officer as long as you keep writing letters to her every few weeks. I am proud of you, even if I do not always show it.

Love,

Mom

PS — I will be out with my date until at least midnight tonight. If you need me, I will have my cell phone on. I am sure you and Laurie will be fine, though. Behave!

PPS — I bought bagels and Philadelphia cream cheese (ha-ha) for tomorrow morning's breakfast. I look forward to catching up with Laurie.

"See?" Laurie said. "Your mom loves you. Plus she's not trying to pump out a replacement baby."

I didn't have a reply for that, so I just kind of patted Laurie on the arm. She dropped her bag on the couch in the living room, and we walked out into the cold setting sun, our arms reloaded with chips, dips, cups, plates, candy, cheese, crackers, and even little noisemakers for Sol and company.

At the home, there were pathetic little decorations up for the occasion, to supplement the lame-o Christmas tree from the week before, which was one of those artificial jobs that they create to give the illusion of a real, yet sickly, one. Why wouldn't they just make a healthy-looking plastic tree? They also had a dorky electric menorah, so the Jewish patients wouldn't feel left out of the overly commercial and transparently manufactured good cheer. And, of course, now they had added the horns and streamers so the fogies could celebrate a new year of captivity.

I was in a weird mood, I guess. Laurie has always been one of those people who can just shrug off their sadness at will, though, so she jumped right into the party spirit. While I was gloomily filling cups with bright blue juice at the nurses' station counter, she was getting Sol up out of bed for a hug. It was incredible: Here was this guy who hadn't been able to walk three steps a few days before, and within seconds, she had him hustling from room to room inviting everyone out to the nurses' station. She even gave Claudelle a CD to put into their little boom box. I don't know where she got it, but it was this *Christmas with the Rat Pack* disk, which had nothing but Frank Sinatra and his buddies singing holiday tunes. Sol was almost dancing along, and the other residents were emerging from their rooms with smiles on. Laurie even got Mrs. Goldfarb out of her room a second time, after Sol had temporarily convinced her that she wasn't wearing pants. Within moments, everyone was munching, drinking, and shuffling feet along with the music. God knows how, but Laurie even convinced Sol and a few others to put on cone-shaped party hats that she had produced from somewhere.

Even I had to admit two things:

— Laurie was good at this stuff

and

— This wasn't such a painful way to spend New Year's Eve.

I was almost starting to feel rather cheerful myself, right until Sol's fit.

I was chowing down on these little pretzel morsels with cheese and pepperoni in every bite, and Laurie was saying to me, "You know, when you told me your sentence, a hundred hours seemed like forever. Can you believe you're more than halfway done?"

I was about to tell her how I planned to keep on at the home after I finished my mandated time, but a hand on my shoulder stopped me. The hand belonged to an angry Solomon Lewis. "Wait a minute, Alex. You're not a volunteer? I'm your sentence? I'm your PUNISHMENT?"

"Oh, my gosh, Sol. I always assumed you knew. I was assigned to spend a hundred hours here by the juvenile court, with the patient of my mom's choice. She picked you because she said we would be a good match."

"So now I'm a charity case, heh? I never thought I would live to see the day when I would be a burden for the state to put on somebody else's back."

"It's not like that. They thought I could learn from you, so I wouldn't . . . um, you know . . . get arrested again."

"What in the world did they arrest a clean-cut boy like you for anyway?"

"Well, it was nothing, really."

"Nothing? Like what kind of nothing? Jaywalking? Skipping school to be with your darling, here?"

"No, I . . . I got drunk and tried to drive my mom's car to my dad's house. But it was no big deal. Really."

"No big deal? You didn't hit anybody?"

"No, I didn't hit anybody. Well, except a lawn gnome."

"A lawn gnome, you hit? So you drove up on somebody's lawn?"

"Well, yeah, but . . ."

"And this is the 'no big deal'? You're lucky to be alive, Alex. And you're lucky that you DIDN'T kill anyone. 'No big deal,' he says. You're even more *meshuggeh* than I thought."

"But . . ."

"Just get out of here, you little criminal. Old I might be, and sick I might be, but handouts from a crazy outlaw who doesn't even know how stupid he is, I don't need."

I was stunned. I noticed that the music had stopped, and the whole roomful of people had turned to stare at me. Laurie put her hand on my arm, but I shrugged it off and walked out.

The last thing I heard was Laurie saying to Sol, "You know, that wasn't fair. He really isn't as bad as you . . ."

Then the elevator door closed behind me, and I was headed for the lobby. It occurred to me that I was still holding a little plate of food and a Dixie cup of juice. Leave it to me to get shouted out of a New Year's party, at a nursing home no less, and make my dramatic exit, dateless, with snacks in hand. Oh, well. If you're going to look like the biggest goober on the planet, you might as well wash down the lump in your throat with some nice cheese curls.

When I got home, the light on our machine was

blinking with a message from Laurie's cell phone: "Come back, Alex, all is forgiven. Stop being such a drama queen! Sol is even sorry. Aren't you, Sol?" She must have held the phone out to him, but all I could hear was a cough, and then a quick, "Get your little car-crashing *tuchis* back here before I..." At that point, Laurie hung up in a hurry.

There was no way I was going back there. By the time I hiked all the way to the bus, all the way back to the home, and all the way upstairs, all the fogies would be popping out their teeth, whisking off their wigs, and settling down for their sponge baths. It was much better all around if I took a nice shower, changed into raggedy old sweats, nuked some pop-corn, and sat on the sofa for hours watching all the people with lives wishing each other a happy new year on TV.

But after my l-o-n-g shower, the machine light was blinking a whole bunch of times. I pushed PLAY with that sense of dread you'd get if you pissed off a karate master who had a key to your house. Sure enough, the messages got progressively worse. After the third one — "All right, wuss boy, I'm on my way over there, and I'm all pumped up to jump on you and start working your head like a speed bag" — I just hit DELETE eleven or twelve times, and waited for the invasion.

Which came as soon as I curled up in an old throw blanket and settled in to watch the MTV Beach Party Unplugged Cribs TRL New Year's Rockin' Eve Bash. There was a rattling of keys, a turning of tumblers, and a whoosh of cold air. I was afraid to look, but the deceptively small-sounding footsteps were coming up behind me. Then Laurie did her famous somersault couch flip, landing just opposite me with her feet up on my legs. She took a long look at me — the mop of damp, uncontrollable hair, the popcorn bucket held protectively on my chest, and the tragic little-boy frown that had saved me from her wrath a thousand times, minimum — and reached into the bucket. She scrunched up so her face was inches from mine, blew her bangs out of her eyes, and said, "You're too pathetic to kill. Hand me the remote, will ya? Before I change my mind."

We had a pretty good night being pals, as long as I didn't think about my mom being out on a date when I wasn't, or Sol evicting me from the home, or the warmth of Laurie's legs on mine. We watched the New Year's countdown shows and played Monopoly at the same time, while I ignored the blatant cheating that Laurie always referred to as her "little bank errors." As payback, Laurie lent me money to buy back my properties when they went bankrupt again and again. Just once it would be cool to think that Laurie wasn't nine steps ahead of me at any given moment, but hey — you can't have everything. When there were only ten minutes left until midnight, Laurie finally allowed herself to finish me off in the game, and we went to the kitchen to make egg creams. An egg cream isn't as gross as it sounds. It's a New York thing: First you pour chocolate or vanilla syrup into a tall glass, then you pour in milk, then you spritz in some seltzer really fast and whip a spoon around in there. What you get is essentially chocolate (or vanilla) milk, but with an extra zap of fizzy goodness. Well, whatever you might think of the egg-cream concept, the point is that Laurie and I have been making them as a late-night snack beverage since Bill Clinton was president, and we aren't ready to stop yet.

By the time we were done pouring, pouring, spritzing, stirring, sipping, and cleaning up, it was 11:59. We stood very, very close together in the living room and watched the ball fall over Times Square. At the big "Happy New Year!" moment, we clinked glasses and drank. Then Laurie wiped some chocolate froth off of my lip with one finger, and we stared into each other's eyes through the whole obligatory "Auld Lang Syne" saxophone serenade. At what I thought was the exactly, precisely perfect instant, I leaned toward her, suavely raised one eyebrow, and made my voice low and gravelly: "How about a new year's kiss?" She laughed, said, "In your dreams, buddy boy," and punched me in the arm, hard.

This prompted an outbreak of pillow-related violence, which was only quelled when I missed Laurie's head with a mighty overhand clout and accidentally shattered both our egg cream glasses. By the time we tweezed the last glass shard out of the carpet and threw a towel on the floor to sop up most of the brown, gooey stain, we were both feeling tired. So we set up our sleeping bags, did all our toothbrushing-type-stuff, and lay down in the living room between the TV and the chocolate-coated rug disaster area. I was just drifting off to sleep when Laurie reached over and put her arm around me. She murmured, "You know, Sol really likes you a lot, buddy. G'night," and rolled back away from me. She fell asleep like she always does, almost instantaneously. But I was still lying there, half out of it, trying to ignore the loud *tick, tick, tick* of our kitchen clock and the ghost of Laurie's arm on my shoulder, when the front door opened.

I didn't open my eyes, but I didn't have to. My mom had that loud whisper people use when they're doing a really miserable job of being quiet, and she was only fifteen feet away. "Ssshhhhh!" she said, "They're asleep."

Then a man's voice answered: "I see them. What the hell is that splotch on the rug next to them, though?"

I had a question, too: What was my dad doing here with my mom at two A.M.?

HAPPy NEW yEAR!

Okay, I admit it: I employed the "fake sleep" trick, at least until the murmur of my parents' voices eventually blended into the strange language of dreams. The next thing I knew, it was morning, and Laurie was desperately spraying vast quantities of carpet cleaners on the chocolate amoeba that had nearly swallowed the room. "Funny," I remarked. "The stain didn't look so big last night."

"Well, now it looks like one of those giant oil spills in Alaska. I keep expecting a flock of endangered herons to come staggering out from under the towel and die at my feet."

Hey, there's an image to drown out any ugly thoughts I might be having about my parental units.

I dove right in and helped with the cleanup by spraying even more bluish gunk all over everything (which, by the way, why IS every liquid cleaner some shade of blue-green? Just wondering.). Pretty soon, the stain was mostly a lovely fluorescent greenish-brownish gray, if that's a color. And the smell was like what you'd get if you dumped a tub of toilet tank fresheners into a vat of melted Hershey's Kisses. Just then, my mom stomped down from upstairs, took one whiff, and fled back up with a hand over her mouth. I had that "she'll be back" feeling, though.

Boy, am I smart. About ten minutes later, while Laurie and I were feverishly brainstorming for either a solution or an excuse, Mom came down again, with a sheepish dad in tow. We stopped trying to figure out a way to smuggle the entire roomful of carpeting out of the house, and started wishing we'd smuggled OURSELVES out instead.

Since my social skills are so finely honed, I broke the ice. "Hi, Dad. Did somebody put the city of Philadelphia upstairs without my noticing?" The 'rents looked at each other, and I noticed they were — ugh! — holding hands. This was an unusual scene, to say the least.

"Well, we . . . that is, I . . . your mother . . . uh . . ."

"OK, Dad. Thanks for clarifying. Mom?"

"Can we talk about this later, Alex? Like maybe after some breakfast? After all, we have company here!"

We sure do, I thought. "All right, Mom. Let's eat."

"But wait, Alex. What's that stain on the carpet?"

I smiled like a choirboy. "Stain? Oh, you mean THAT little dot on the rug? I'll be glad to explain it to you after all the COMPANY leaves."

So we sat down to the ABC special: awkwardness, bagels, and coffee. All of which went down great with the lingering disinfectant and chocolate fumes. Laurie kicked me under the table and rolled her eyes as my parents chatted like two people who hadn't just spent twelve months and thirty thousand bucks battling each other tooth and nail through the legal system. I rubbed my shin and made faces back at her behind my coffee mug. When she got up to get more cream cheese, I caught myself checking out her legs again, and immediately made my first New Year's resolution: NO SCOPING LAURIE! And I didn't break that one for a good five minutes, although my parents must have been breaking their own resolutions left and right. Whatever. Laurie ate in a hurry, and didn't say anything else until it was time to say good-bye to my parents:

"Bye, Mrs. G. Bye, Mr. G. I have to go work out at the dojo. Thanks for breakfast. Sorry about the rug!"

Off she went, looking chipper. Sure, she was feeling good — she was off to karate-kick things just for fun, and I wanted to karate-kick my parents, but couldn't do that OR have fun. Plus, I still had to cope with this weirdness, and the rug issue. "Hey, Mom, Dad. What's going on?"

Oh, no. Dad put down his coffee mug, and pinched the bridge of his nose between his finger and thumb. Mom took a big swig of orange juice, pushed aside her glass, and nervously pulled her hair back away from her face. It had been a while since I had seen these signals, but they were instantly familiar, and I knew a Big Talk was coming. It's always been exactly the same: When my grandfather got sick for the last time, when I asked my day care teacher why the classroom goldfish was floating faceup, when I did the little skateboard-roof thing — Dad pinches the nose and Mom does the hair pullback. Plus, the longer and more elaborate the pinching and pullbacking are, the worse the talk is going to be.

So this time, when Dad fiddled with his nose for about half a minute until I was ready for his skin to start blistering from the friction, and Mom pulled her hair back so tight it looked like she had just gotten face-lift surgery, I knew this Big Talk would be a doozy.

"Honey, do you remember yesterday morning, when I was a bit upset?"

"Uh, Mom, do you remember the *Titanic* movie, when the ship hit a bit of ice?"

"Okay, fine, a lot upset. That was because your father and I had a long argument about his moving to Philadelphia. Then we agreed to have dinner and talk it over last night. There was this jazz trio playing in the corner of the restaurant, and they played our wedding song, and one thing led to another . . ."

"Stop right there, Mom. I don't need to hear any more, especially when I just ate. So you're telling me

Dad paid these guys to serenade you, and you took it as a sign from God that you should get back together?"

"It wasn't like that, Alex. Was it, Simon?"

"Well . . ."

Mom took that moment to demonstrate her unique mood-switching abilities: "Wait, you PAID them to play that song? You SET ME UP?"

Oh, boy. Now things felt back to normal.

"Yes, Janet, I did."

Mom took a deep breath and held it. So did Dad. I felt an instant cold sweat bursting out all over my back. Then Mom reached over and squeezed Dad's hand on the table. "Thank you, Simon. That was really sweet!"

Wow, a double mood switch! I give up. Maybe things were NEVER normal in this family.

But Mom never stopped trying for normalcy, anyway: "Now, Alex, about that stain . . ."

ENTER THE CHA-KINGS

On January 2, which was a Tuesday, we went back to school. In homeroom, I was talking with Laurie about my problem with Sol when inspiration struck me like a ham-sized fist. Well, actually a ham-sized fist struck me like an inspiration. Or something. I got punched, and inspired. Here's how it happened.

"Laurie," I was saying, "how am I going to show up at Sol's place today? What am I supposed to say?"

"I already told you he's not mad. That's just how he is — he blows off some steam once in a while."

"Oh, like you're the big expert on Solomon Lewis all of a sudden, O feet-washing genius."

"Don't get mad at me just because you befriended an old man under false pretenses. I'm just trying to tell you things will be okay, that's all."

And then came the fist, bashing into my right upper arm with three hundred pounds of semi-blubbery football player behind it. Bryan Gilson. "Hey, Lawn Boy. I missed you over the break. Why didn't you come to Jody Krasiloff's New Year's party? Oh, that's right, it's because you're a complete loser who's grounded for life."

He sat down on the edge of my desk while I struggled desperately against the urge to rub my arm where he'd clobbered me.

"Anyway, I couldn't help overhearing that you got your geezer friend mad at you. Since I know you'll go to jail if you blow off your probation, and since homeroom wouldn't be the same without your sorry company, I'll give you some free advice."

Laurie was never much for staying quiet. "Free advice from you? You just learned to speak in sentences like, last week, and Alex needs YOUR wisdom? Anyway, he's trying to stay OUT of trouble, which isn't exactly your specialty. Why don't you go impress your friends by walking away AND chewing gum?"

"No, really. All you have to do, dorkwad, is make the old man feel special. You know, like, bring him a gift. The severed head of a lawn gnome, maybe?"

I crossed my eyes and pretended to think about

it for a second. Then I really DID think about it for a second. Then I got an amazing idea, just as the bell rang for first period. I grabbed Bryan's hand and shook it profusely. "That's IT! You ARE smarter than your girlfriend told me you were last night! Thanks, Bryan. I owe you one."

As I ran off in triumph, Bryan and Laurie were shrugging at each other, trying to figure out why I was so excited. It was like a little pixie-bison bonding moment.

Bryan's "advice" had actually given me a great idea. This idea was amazing on about seventeen different levels:

1. It would impress the judge with my apparent selflessness and personal growth.

2. It would entertain and amuse dozens of oldsters.

3. It would make my mom think I might have some shred of redeemable goodness.

4. It was a chance to play guitar.

5. It might even shut Sol up for an hour.

Okay, so it was only amazing for five reasons. Still, they were mighty big reasons. The idea was this: I would stage a benefit jazz concert at the home, with profits going toward future cultural events there. It would help people, and might even prove to Sol that he wasn't just my "punishment." It was a win-win situation all around. And I knew exactly the people I would need to make it happen.

The Cha-KINGS. These were two members of my high school jazz band. Steven was a superhuman drummer, and his eterna-girlfriend Annette was a hellaciously gifted piano whiz. I called them the *Cha-KINGS* after the sound that happens in a science-fiction movie when two spaceships' airlocks are slammed together by the nearly irresistible force of a magnetic tractor beam: *cha-KING*. That's how close Steven and Annette were. I needed the Cha-KINGS for this project because of the three things they loved nearly as much as they adored each other, which were jazz, being do-gooders, and their constant quest to create the perfect benefit concert.

Why were they so into benefit concerts? Well, the obvious reason was that the concerts they put on together always involved playing jazz and do-gooding. But there was more to it: Three years ago, they had fallen in love while planning and rehearsing a benefit concert to pay the hospital bills for Steven's little brother, Jeffrey, who had cancer. Even though Annette never got to play a single note at the concert, and Steven had to run out during intermission to take Jeffrey to the hospital, the gig was a huge success. The bills got paid, Jeffrey became the unofficial town mascot, a position he holds to this day, and of course Steven and Annette got each other.

Really, it's so sweet I could hurl.

The Cha-KINGS are A students, of course. They are the most beloved couple ever to walk the halls of a high school without wearing athletic uniforms. They are jaw-droppingly good musicians. And they are very, very nice. Kind to animals. Honor Society officers. Patron saints of the Key Club. Very, very different from the mediocre guitarist, the car-thieving lawn-gnome mangler, the convicted delinquent who would now be attempting to enlist their aid.

Good thing I'm so charming.

Oh, who was I kidding? These people LIVED for benefit concerts. If Steven's mom were choking on a chicken bone, he would start the Heimlich maneuver while Annette started designing the poster for "Bone Aid." They would jump on this opportunity. It was in the bag.

Right?

I thought about my approach all day. We all had jazz band practice right after school, and then I would be heading straight for the home. So if I did this right, I would have the news of the concert ready as ammunition for when I had to face Sol. I decided to leave my last class early, because Steven and Annette had an independent-study music class at the end of the day. That's how amazing these people's lives were: They had convinced an entire high school to give them a special daily period built for two. As for me, I had to practically promise my firstborn child to my precalc teacher just so I could miss the last eight minutes of his valuable instructional droning.

So there I was, on the long hallway approaching the band room. As I got closer I could hear the tinkling of Annette's piano, along with something else: like a *clink, clink* sound, but with different pitches, and beautiful. I peeked in the little square window of the door, and saw Annette playing chords, while this complicated single-note line of clinks was floating over the top. It hit me that I knew the melody: "Sunrise, Sunset." Well, that was fitting. Steven was playing the marimba, which is like a big xylophone thing with wooden bars instead of the metal kind. I hadn't even known he played anything other than drums — I hadn't even known our school had a marimba — but I guess that's why he and Annette were music gods while I was sitting on my *tuchis* in math class. I poked my head in the door, feeling a bit weird about breaking in on the musical dance they had going, especially when Steven suddenly started embellishing the melody with all sorts of fast little grace notes that I wouldn't have been able to pull off on the guitar, much less on a second instrument.

Annette was talking and playing at the same time, just in case her powers hadn't already been awesome enough. "Okay, Steven, that sounds great for the melody. Now, do you think you can add in the harmony line?"

I was thinking, *Duh. How can he play extra harmony notes when he only has two mallets?* But then he did this amazing thing: He picked up an extra mallet for each hand, without even missing a beat, and kind of spread the mallets between different fingers, so now it was like he was holding upside-down chopsticks or something. And sure enough, he started playing the melody and a harmony part at the same time. Finally, just when the insane skill level of these people was nearly too depressing to contemplate, he reached behind him to a xylophone that was set up there, and finished his solo with one hand jamming away on each instrument.

Annette and Steven gave each other a little grin

at the last note of the solo, and then — in perfect unison — burst into the little coda that ends the *Fiddler on the Roof* medley. When they stopped, I applauded. Annette turned to Steven and said, "Show-off!"

"Wait, he wasn't showing off THAT much. I kept waiting for him to light his mallets on fire and start juggling them during the solo, or play bass drum with his foot or something."

They both just kind of stared at me like they had caught me beating a baby seal or something. I had forgotten that the Cha-KINGS are SERIOUS ABOUT MUSIC. "Oh, well. Maybe next time." More staring. "Hi, guys. You're probably wondering why I'm here. I mean, why I'm here *now*, instead of after the bell rings. I mean, instead of in math. Because that's what I have now. Math. Precalc. Uh . . ." Still more staring.

"Would the two of you like to help some elderly people in need?"

Their eyes lit up. For a babbling idiot, I'm a pretty good salesman.

HOME AGAIN

I walked into Sol's room that evening with good news and sweaty palms. I know Laurie had said Sol wasn't mad at me, but she was only ALMOST always right. He wasn't around, so I sat down in the chair and thought about the afternoon. Steven and Annette had surprised me a little bit; they didn't think we could pull off a successful benefit concert without months of lead time, so we had agreed on just practicing for a few weeks and doing an informal, free concert at the home. They had also gotten me to commit to practicing every Monday and Wednesday afternoon until 4:30, which they apparently did anyway just for fun like the mutants they were. So now I REALLY had no life, even if having no life with two other people and my guitar was better than having no life alone in my house.

Although it occurred to me that HAVING a life would beat both of my options.

Just when I might have started to get depressed

about the sorry state of my social status, I heard a resonant "HOO-hah!" from the elevator area. A few seconds later, Sol came in and the fun began.

"Hey, look! It's Mr. Um, my compulsory volunteer. Happy new year. Did you have a nice New Year's Eve after you abandoned me to the lonely fate of the forgotten and the elderly?"

"Listen, Sol, I'm sorry I ran out, and I'm sorry I never explained why I was here. But I thought you KNEW."

"Alex, Alex. You'll learn one day that real apologies don't come with a BUT in the middle. In the meantime, thank you. Are you going to maybe play for me today?"

"No, but I've got big news. In a few weeks, I'm putting on a jazz concert here, for everyone who wants to come."

"YOU'RE putting on a concert? With what musicians?"

"Well, there are these two kids at my school who are like prodigies or something. There's a drummer named Steven and a piano player named Annette. And I'll play guitar. I think it will be great."

"Great, I don't know about. But it should be more entertaining than sitting around waiting for my breathing treatment, and wondering whether anybody pished in the hydrotherapy pool."

"Wow, thanks for your enthusiasm."

Sol is either totally immune to sarcasm, or so good at counter-sarcasm that I can never even tell whether he's making fun of me. "Don't mention it, *boychik*. But I hope you know how much work it is putting on a show."

"What do you mean? I've played in shows before. We'll practice, we'll show up, and we'll play, right?"

"Well, maybe. If you have the room reserved. And if you have permission to get your event put on the schedule. And if the cheap bastards who run this place are willing to pay all the overtime for the orderlies to get us all down there and back up. AND if you have all the power you need, and microphones, and extension cords, speakers, lights . . ."

Perhaps it would have been a good idea to ask how he knew so much about this stuff. But I had already used up my good idea for the day. "I get the point, Sol. Don't worry, I'll get it all done. Trust me."

"Heh. 'Trust me,' he says. My grandmother always used to tell me, *'Nisht azoi gich macht zich vi es tracht zich.'*"

"And that would mean . . . ?"

"Easier said than done, *boychik*. Easier said than done."

"Uh, okay Sol, there's another thing I wanted to talk about today. I'm really not a criminal or anything. The only reason I got in trouble was because, well, my parents are divorced, and my mom was going out on a date, so I took my mom's car and . . ."

"Wait a minute. What about the drinking?"

"Okay, I was drinking. But . . ."

"You see, Alex, again with the 'but.' But, but, but. Always with the but. A criminal, you're not. You might even be a nice boy. But you did something wrong, and you got caught. That's all I need to know. Everything else is just excuses."

"But . . ."

"See?"

"Aaarrrggghhh! You're so frustrating!"

"I know. Thank God I'm also handsome, or who knows how I would have gotten along in the world?"

January 3

Dear Judge Trent,

I am pleased to report a new breakthrough in my community service work. Much as I enjoy serving Mr. Lewis, I have come to realize that I could do even more if I set my mind to it. In light of this, I have decided to arrange and perform a concert of Mr. Lewis's beloved jazz music for the entire resident population at the home. I feel that this will provide an enjoyable cultural experience for the community members there, and also give Mr. Lewis something to look forward to as he recovers from some recent health difficulties he has experienced.

I told Mr. Lewis of my plan the other day, and he appeared enthusiastic. In just one visit, he wished me a happy new year, told me I was a nice boy, AND

said the concert could be, and I quote, "entertaining."
Yes, I suppose you could say we are really bonding
now.

Thank you for a wonderful growth opportunity.
Sincerely,
Alex Gregory

PS — There are only forty-two hours remaining in
my sentence. Have you considered my earlier request
to extend my time at the home? I really think Sol
would miss me if I stopped visiting him.

AM I A GREAT MUSICIAN, OR WHAT?

MY first practice session with Steven and Annette was like being dragged around by a fast horse. Adding to my pleasure was the fact that Laurie was going to show up at some point to watch us. Because, let's face it, if there was a possibility that I might be humiliated completely, Laurie wanted to be in the front row.

While we got set up with our instruments, I told Steven and Annette what I wanted us to play, basically a bunch of the easiest songs we already did in jazz band. Between the time crunch and the fact that both Steven and Annette were so much better than I was, I figured simple was good. Both of them agreed that the list would work, so we were ready to go. They looked at me. Annette said, "Hey, Alex, call the first tune."

"Uh, how about 'Mercy, Mercy, Mercy'?"

They both took out the chart and put it on their music stands. Then they started giving me that "you are an idiot" look — Sol had once referred to it as "the fish eye" — again. Steven asked me, in the same voice that kindergarten teachers use with their slowest pupils, "Aren't you going to count it off?"

It's weird being in charge. "Sure. One — two — three — four." We started playing, but I knew right away something was wrong. Annette stopped.

"That's too fast, Alex. This song is supposed to have a groove."

Oh, excuse me, Hipster Girl. "Sorry. One — two — three — four."

Annette was right. The new tempo was better. Steven had this whole laid-back backbeat going on; Annette was doing a cool bass line with her left hand, and chording with her right. I had the melody, and thought I was actually doing a good job with it. Then we got to the solo section, and all hell broke loose. First Annette soloed while I just played the chords, which should have been easy enough. But then she started playing these funky accents all over the place, and somehow I lost the beat. It was like when you're trying to remember a number and your friend purposely yells out random sequences of digits to mess you up.

Well, Annette messed me up. When she realized I was totally lost, she glanced over and said, "eighteen-two-three-four, nineteen-two-three-four," so I'd know what measure we were up to. Five bars later, it was Steven's turn to make me look like a goon. All of a sudden, Annette was playing the chords again, so I switched over to the melody. But just as I was attempting to get my feel back, Steven started doing all these weird odd-time rolls on the toms, with quick little offbeat accents on the cymbals. I almost counted my way through the chaos by concentrating on the steady *boom-boom* of the bass drum, until he started messing around with that, too.

It was hopeless. I was lost in a vast, storm-tossed sea of shifting rhythmic complexities. Of course, at my instant of deepest confusion, Laurie walked in. So she got to see Steven whisper to me cuttingly, "Psst! DROP OUT!" I stopped playing, and Steven and Annette continued, playfully turning the rest of the song into a drum-and-piano conversation. He would play a rhythm, she would play it back at him. She would do a tinkling little run on the high notes, he would somehow echo it instantly on the bells of his cymbals. He would go nuts with his bass drum, she would suddenly fire back a flurry of wacky low notes. I was just sitting there, cradling my guitar in my lap. Laurie was shaking her head at the scene. And then, suddenly, Steven and Annette were playing the main theme of the song in perfect unison, and the song ended with a perfect fade-out. Laurie applauded, I glared. Everyone's eyes were on me. I had to say something.

"Well, that one shows promise. What's next?"

"You're kidding, right? We need to do that one again from the top. Right, Steven?"

"Yeah. But maybe we should play simpler this time, until . . ."

"Until what? Until I develop mental telepathy like you guys have?"

"No, just until you learn the music. Are you always this touchy?"

Laurie had to pipe up. "Why, yes, Steven, he is."

So we took it from the top. Again and again. Until I was practically begging for some "Mercy, Mercy, Mercy" myself. But we did get to the point where I could play through the song without completely self-destructing, which was a plus. We ran through a couple of other songs, too, and I managed to fool myself into believing that I was really holding my own. At the end of the rehearsal, Annette gave me a list of things she thought I should focus on while practicing at home. I was thinking, *Wow, and I thought Laurie was bossy. How does Steven stand it?* But they seemed so happy together, and I had the dating record of a leper, so maybe I was missing something.

On the walk home, I kept waiting for Laurie to bust on me about my performance, but she was in a really contemplative mood. Every once in a while this happened, like the time she made me camp out in her backyard when we were nine and we made up stories about the stars until we both fell asleep. Or once at the beach, when she started wondering whether there were two other kids in Europe or Africa watching these same waves rolling away from their beach. Tonight's food for thought was whether it was possible to be happily married.

"Alex, do you think your parents are going to stay together this time?"

"I don't know, why?"

"Well, I was just thinking about it. I mean, won't the same stuff that drove them apart the first time just drive them apart again?"

"It depends, I guess. I'm not even sure what the problem was in the first place — but maybe they're different now. Don't you think people can change for the better if they want to?"

"I'm not sure. My mom was a miserable wife and mother for us, but now she's trying again with a new husband. So SHE must think she's changed."

"Unless she just thinks it was all your dad's fault, and she'll be the perfect mate for your stepdad."

"You know, Alex, she probably IS the perfect

mate for my stepdad — they're both idiots!" She got quiet for a minute, and then blew the hair out of her eyes. "Men and women CAN be happy together, though, right? I mean, somehow, somewhere?"

"Sure, Laur. Look at Steven and Annette. *I* think she orders him around so much, she should have given him a tip at the end of the rehearsal, but he must love something about her."

"Alex, can I ask you something?"

"Just did."

"Ha-ha. Do you think Annette is pretty?"

I wanted to shout, "You're prettier!" But you never know how Laurie is going to respond to a statement like that, and there's always that "sudden use of karate" problem she tends to have. So I just said, "Yeah, I guess so. I mean, in a band-geek kind of way. Why?"

"I dunno. Steven just looks at her like she hung the moon or something. I think it would be great if a guy looked at me that way. I could see staying together for life with somebody who cared about me that much."

"*I* care about you that much." Oops, dang! Did I say that out loud?

"Yeah, but I mean a real guy."

I must have had some facial reaction to that one, because Laurie backtracked. "I mean, you're a real guy, and you're good-looking and nice to me and funny and . . . umm . . . I dunno, great. But you're my ALEX. You know?"

"Yeah, I suppose so." But I was a little hurt anyway. "You know who I think is REALLY hot? That girl Stephanie Simon, from homeroom."

"The snotty cheerleader? For real?"

"Oh, yes. Absolutely for real."

"You don't think she's a little — I don't know — trashy with the tight clothes and everything?"

"Sure, but she has other good points, too."

"Chuckle, chuckle. And don't you think her face is a little odd-looking?"

"Stephanie Simon has a face? I don't think I ever noticed that before. Huh, who knew?"

At that point, I knew the chop was coming. But I couldn't stop it. That's why Laurie had a black belt and I just had lots of bruises. But when Laurie hit me this time, it felt extra-hard, even for her. "OOWWW!"

"Oh, it hurts when I do that? Huh, who knew?" We were in front of Laurie's house at that point, so she just flounced away up her driveway, leaving me to wonder how we had gone from a philosophical discussion to me getting pounded on in just a few short blocks. I watched her until she got inside. Just before she shut the door, she stuck out her tongue at me. Which is weird, because whatever had just happened, I was pretty certain she had started it.

January 26

Dear Judge Trent,

It is with the greatest pleasure that I humbly extend my invitation for you to attend the first-ever Egbert P. Johnson Memorial Home for the Aged Winter Jazz Thingie, an event that will have a fancier title as soon as I think of one. This will be a spectacular concert, featuring me on guitar, and precocious jazz geniuses Steven Alper and Annette Watson on drums and piano, respectively. The festivities will begin promptly at six P M Eastern Standard Time on February 7, at the recreation hall on the first floor of the home.

I would relish the opportunity to demonstrate to you the sincerity and strength of my newfound enthusiasm for assisting the elderly, as well as my organizational and musical skills.

If it is not too much trouble, please let me know as soon as possible whether you will be attending, so that I may reserve you a seat of honor in the front between my mother, with whom you are acquainted, and my good friend, Mr. Solomon Lewis.

Thank you.

Yours truly,

Alex Gregory

January 30

Dear Alex,

Your concert sounds like a wonderful event, as well as a marvelous learning experience for all involved. However, I am afraid I have to decline your invitation to attend, due to some unfinished private business of my own.

I look forward to hearing of your great success in this worthy endeavor.

Sincerely,

Judge J. Trent

A NIGHT FOR SURPRISES

The month of January was a mind-numbing slog through hell. I had practice with the Cha-KINGS two days a week and visits with Sol on the in-between days. On the weekends, even if I hadn't been grounded, I would have had to ground myself to study for my midterms, which were the last week of the month. My parents were now officially "dating" each other, which was odd and icky, so I just tried to completely ignore it, although at least my dad seemed to have forgotten about moving to Philadelphia for the time being. Oh, and to top it all off, things were awkward and strange with Laurie. I really wanted my old pal, Laurie, back, so we could laugh and make egg creams, get kicked out of the mall restaurants together, and just generally hang. But instead I had this weird new Laurie, who smiled less, battered me more, and still somehow made me think of her constantly. I was tired all the time, and my dreams were a terrifying jumble of random, out-of-tune guitar noises, massive precalc problems, scrambled American history factoids, and images of my parents and Laurie; Sol and Laurie; Annette, Steven, and Laurie.

With some extra Laurie thrown in for good luck.

Somehow, I made it through the month, passed my midterms, and staggered into my last practice before the concert. I even remembered my guitar and sheet music, which I thought was a nice touch. The Cha-KINGS were all set up, but had an odd, almost guilty expression on their usually eager faces. Annette dropped the bomb: "Alex, first of all, we want to thank you very much for the opportunity you have offered us to play at the home tomorrow. It's always nice to be given a chance to help people, and you know we both love playing music. But . . ." She stopped talking and straightened out her very preppy band-geek skirt. It was hard to believe, but Annette seemed, well, nervous.

"Okay, but?"

"Uh . . . we don't think you're really ready to play with us tomorrow. Steven knows his parts cold, and I certainly have a handle on what I'm doing, but your playing is still not really where it should be."

"I'm doing okay. We'll get through the concert. Listen, just last Tuesday, you said my solo on the Fiddler medley was 'nice,' and I haven't gotten lost and had to drop out of anything for at least a week."

Steven took his potshot at the rapidly deflating target formerly known as my ego. "Alex, you're doing OKAY. But we want better than just OKAY. We want GREAT. We want EXCELLENT. And even though you've been trying much harder than I'd thought you could, you're just . . . not . . . quite . . . there. I'm sorry."

"Wait a minute. Annette, Steven, listen to me. All of those people at the home, they're depending on us. They've been looking forward to this for weeks. They don't have much going on in their lives, and they need a little inspiration. Maybe we could bring a smile to their faces. Who knows? Maybe our little concert could even help somebody to . . . hey, wait. Why are you laughing?"

Laurie popped up from behind the piano, and growled, "Gotcha!" Actually, it was a pretty respectable imitation of Sol, although I was NOT pleased that Laurie had added this newest weapon to her arsenal of Alex-torture methods. "Wow, Alex, you sounded like a guy who *cares* for a moment there. It scared me."

Steven and Annette were cracking up now. I had always thought the Cha-KINGS were stiff and dull, but I guess you can just add that to my long list of misjudgments. "I DO care!" And I did. I mean, Laurie had a point. I used to not care. And Sol still bugged me, and irritated me, and even got me furious pretty much every time. But I wanted this concert to go right.

Annette said, "We know, Alex. Just because we're the Cha-KINGS doesn't mean we can't tell when a person is serious about a project. Don't worry, we're going to play the job. How could we miss it? Laurie told us your friend Sol is the most entertaining man on earth."

Wait just one cotton-pickin' minute! They *knew*

I called them the Cha-KINGS? I was going to KILL Laurie. Right until she took the surprise cake out from behind her back.

"Congratulations, Alex. You're really going to pull this thing off. And it will be an event to remember."

Laurie was right, too, although not quite in any way we could have imagined. The concert was a success in all the ways you'd want. The stage got set up. The orderlies transported everyone to the right place at the right time. The oldsters loved the music. Steven and Annette got a big kick out of playing. My parents sat together in the front row with Laurie and Sol, and didn't make any kind of fighting scene whatsoever. And I got through the whole first half of the program without any major embarrassments.

I admit, I was a little tense at the start of the show. The big manager lady of the home said a few words about how wonderful it was to see young people being active in the community, blah blah blah. Then she handed the microphone to me. I had been so focused on the musical part that it never crossed my mind that I'd have to speak in public, too. I looked at my mom and dad, who were leaning forward a bit, waiting to hear my brilliant words. I looked at Sol, who was coughing hard into a napkin, totally oblivious to the onstage festivities. I looked at Laurie, who was crossing her eyes and sticking her tongue out at me. I took a breath.

"Uh, ladies and gentlemen, thank you for coming today. I mean, not coming exactly, since most of you live here, but . . . well, you know what I mean. Anyway, I'm Alex, and the drummer is Steven. Annette over there is playing piano. Well, she isn't playing piano right NOW, but she will be once I shut up. Okay, here's a song called 'Mercy, Mercy, Mercy.'"

I'm man enough to face the fact that my little blurb wasn't going to win me any speaker-of-the-year awards, but at least I hadn't tripped and fallen off the stage, crushing and killing three elderly jazz fans. Whatever. It was time to play and we did. I could have been looser and more relaxed, but I didn't make any glaring errors. Plus, the Cha-KINGS were so devastatingly skilled that I could probably have been reading my sheet music upside down, playing in the wrong key, and setting my guitar on fire while juggling five enraged cats without anyone particularly noticing. I just basically stayed out of their way, played chords when it was chord time, played melodies when it was my turn to do that, and kept my solos simple. Steven was a subtle tornado. His arms barely even moved, but somehow he played these super-quick fills that always stopped EXACTLY on time. His bass drum danced through the tunes, twining into Annette's bass notes and propelling all of us along with a gliding feel I had never quite heard him achieve before. And Annette. Holy cow! I had once heard Steven say he thought she was most beautiful when she played, and at the time, I hadn't seen it. But she really was striking to watch now. Her fingers had that same light, darting thing going on that Steven's hands did, and her face was totally serene — like she had been born to do this, just exactly this, totally and only *this*. And then once in a while, when she and Steven did one of their mental-telepathy accent runs together, she locked eyes with him in a way that almost made me blush. But instead of blushing, I found myself turning away from Annette to gaze at Laurie.

Okay, I'm making it sound dreamier than it was. For one thing, I was sweating the whole time, sweating like a pig at the International Bacon Festival. For another, I dropped my pick a couple of times, and my music fell off the stand once — which was the one time I was totally sure Sol was watching, because I could hear him clearing his throat like he was covering up one of his little barking laughs as I was frantically reaching down for the pages I'd dropped. And, of course, since it was the home, I kept being conscious of a nearly constant stream of coughing emanating from the audience whenever we got to a quiet part.

But I was feeling pretty good when we walked offstage for intermission after my witty announcement of "We're going to . . . uh . . . take a break now and then . . . um . . . play some more if you're still here." Laurie told me how great she thought it was, the manager gave me a thumbs-up, and my parents smiled and started to walk over to me. But Sol grabbed my arm first. "Alex, I need you to do something for me."

"I'm kind of busy right now, Sol. And I have to play again in a few minutes. Are you having a good time?"

"Sure, sure. You're magnificent, Alex. But can you run up to my room and get my other eyeglasses?"

"What's wrong with the ones you're wearing?"

"They chafe me and I can't see right. If the night nurse hadn't been such a *schmegegge* and moved everything around in my room last night, this wouldn't have happened. Look, would you just go?"

By now, I felt like everyone in America was staring at me, the mean kid who wouldn't get an old man a pair of glasses.

"Fine. Where should I look for them?"

"If I knew where to find them, I would have worn them in the first place. I don't know, they're the only pair of glasses in my room. How hard can it be for a talented young guy like yourself?"

I looked around for Steven and Annette to tell

them where I was going, and that I'd be right back, but they must have run out to the bathroom or something. Laurie saw, and said, "Don't worry, Alex. I'll tell the Cha-KINGS where you went."

I turned to go, just as my clueless father asked Laurie, "What's a Cha-KING?"

Sol's floor was eerily deserted, because everybody was downstairs. It kind of felt like I was in one of those dreams where you show up at your school, and there's nobody in the halls. So it gets darker and darker, and you try to run out, screaming. But it's too late, because a hand reaches out and . . .

Well, anyway, I started to get a little creeped out. In the room, I didn't see anything in the open that looked remotely similar to eyewear. I quickly opened each drawer of Sol's dresser, but no dice there either. By this point, I kept waiting for the inevitable masked killer to grab me, which added to the intensity of my search. I got down to the bottom drawer, which contained nothing but billowing mounds of Sol's underwear — boxers, by the way. I knew the glasses might be beneath the piles in there, but actually moving the boxers was a horrific thought on its own. So I found an unused, wrapped tongue depressor on top of the dresser, popped it open, and sort of stirred the undies around. I hit something solid, and forced myself to reach in. A case! I pulled it out and pushed the little latch device that opened the lid.

But there were no glasses inside, just a big old key. Hmm. Where were the glasses? *Were* there any glasses? Was this a . . . a . . . a trick? *Oh, my God! I* thought. *Sol's up to something. How could I be so gullible?* I launched myself out the door and down the fire stairs, still holding the case. When I came out of the stairwell, my fears became a reality. Okay, not the slaughter ones, but the trickery ones. I could hear Steven's drums start up on a fast Latin tune. When Annette jumped in, I recognized it as a Tito Puente chart called "Para Los Rumberos" that I knew Steven loved. What on earth were they doing?

Then I heard my beloved Tele jumping into action. But I had never played it like this. The notes were rippling forth in a torrent, faster than I would have been on my best day, and with the kind of timing I would have killed for. I came screeching around a corner into the rec room, and saw a tableau I'll never forget. The nurses were up on their feet, swaying. The orderlies were getting down. Even many of the residents were standing and shimmying like people with actual, biological hip joints. And in front of this frenzied hotbed of party power, a man was wailing on MY guitar.

A man whose glasses were chafing him.

Sol looked all the way to the back of the room at me, and mouthed the word that I absolutely knew was coming: "Gotcha!"

What was I going to do? I walked up to the front, and stood between my mom and Laurie, in Sol's seat. Laurie had a huge grin going, and whispered to me, "This is amazing. He's incredible!"

I didn't say a word. I could feel the redness of my face, but Laurie didn't notice. My mom put her arm around my shoulder and said, "Oh, Alex. What a wonderful surprise! I don't know how you did it, but it's like you've brought Mr. Lewis back to life!"

Yeah, excellent. And easy for her to say. She wasn't going to have to get up there and play the guitar when Sol was through demonically possessing it. The song ended to wild applause. I glanced around, and saw that Mrs. Goldfarb was in a state of transformation — she looked like she might write her phone number on an article of clothing and fling it Sol's way if he played much longer. This just kept getting more and more surreal. I decided right then and there that if an MTV film crew rolled up, I was going to hurl myself out the window.

Sol played a few more tunes with Steven and Annette. After his version of the "Fiddler" medley got everyone all misty-eyed, he bowed. Then he walked over to the microphone. Oh, man. Laurie reached over and squeezed my hand. I was sure my miserable scowl and sweaty palm must have been a real turn-on for her, but somehow she resisted sweeping into my arms and kissing me deeply. Short of me getting struck by lightning, I didn't know how the day could have gotten worse.

"Ladies and gentlemen, thank you for your kind

applause. Now I would like to invite back onstage the young man who made this all possible, the real star of today's show — Mr. Alex 'The Um' Gregory!!!"

Everyone clapped, although my puzzled dad had to whisper to my mother, "What's an Um?" Then Sol continued, "Remember to tip your waiters, your waitresses, and bartenders before you leave. That was a joke, Mrs. Goldfarb. Would it kill you to maybe laugh a little? Oh, by the way, folks: Whatever you do, don't let Alex drive you home."

Some people laughed, others looked puzzled. As I took the longest ten-step walk of my life back onto the stage, Sol gave me a weird smile — triumphant and angry at the same time. Then he handed me the guitar. I had a panicked little huddle with Steven and Annette. (Well, I was panicked. They were still all juiced up from the thrill of playing with Sol.) Then I stepped to the mike. "For our last number, we would like to play a little number called 'All Blues.' This is a Miles Davis tune about how it feels to . . . uh . . . play guitar right after Solomon Lewis."

It was the simplest jazz piece I knew, which

would help me get out of this nightmare without too much additional damage. Annette came in on the piano, then Steven started playing a really cool little pattern with his brushes instead of drumsticks, and finally I came in with the parallel sliding melody and harmony lines that move in sixths through a haunting minor scale. Somehow the beauty of the song gradually crept into my bones and I forgot all about the audience, Sol's performance, everything but my fingers slipping up and down the fretboard. Annette played the first solo, which was so good I nearly forgot to keep playing. Then Annette nodded at me, and I burst into my last solo of the night. I did look up at Sol then, and the sadness on his face found its way into the notes I was playing. So did the flash of Laurie's eyes, while the link between my parents' intertwined hands became the elastic lockstep of the harmony. Plus, my anger found its way in there when I played some dissonant clusters of jarring flatted fifths for a few bars. And when I resolved all that tension back into the melody, I wasn't mad anymore. Sure, Sol had showed me up in front of a crowd that included the most important people in my life. But they were surely clapping for me now. If Sol didn't say anything to rub the soreness in, I'd be okay.

And if it got breezy and rainy in the Sahara Desert, they'd change its name to the Sahara Palms Resort.

We finished. People clapped. We packed up. Annette and I helped Steven get his drums out to his mom's car while all of the residents except Sol went back to their floors for the night. After my last trip to carry out my guitar and amp, I walked over to where the Cha-KINGS were chatting with my parents, Laurie, and Sol. Annette said, "Wow, Mr. Lewis, Alex never told me you played."

"I don't play. I haven't played in twenty-seven years and three months. Before that, I played." Sol's words kind of tapered off, and I realized he was very short of breath.

"But you have so much skill. How could you have just given it up?"

"Sweetheart, there's more to life than skill. You're very young. Maybe one day you'll know what I'm talking about."

"But I mean it. You're really brilliant!"

"Thank you." Sol was pale and maybe a little shaky, plus I could tell he didn't want to talk about whatever his secret was. He saw me and changed the subject. "Mr. Um! Did you find my glasses?"

"No, I didn't find your glasses — you don't have another pair of glasses, Sol."

He thought, and breathed, for a moment. "Oh, well, I guess I only have one face anyway. Who needs extra glasses?"

"I found something else, though." I held the key up to the light. "Any idea what it's for?"

"I think maybe one day I'll show you. For now, just keep it very safe." His last few words turned into a titanic cough, and he suddenly sat down on the nearest chair, hard. He was gripping his chest and turning a deep red. A nurse I didn't know appeared out of the blue and called for oxygen. A transport guy shuffled over with a wheelchair that had an air tank attached, and they got Sol into the chair and attached the nose-clip thing to him. Within a couple of moments, while everybody stood around not knowing what to do or say, Sol's color returned and he leaned back in the chair. He turned to me and the orderly and said, "Would you take me upstairs, please? An artist needs his beauty rest. You think I was born looking this lovely?"

I said good-bye to my parents and Laurie. Steven gave me a high five and said, "Some show, huh?" Yup, it had been some show. One way or the other, it had been some show. Annette shook my hand in both of hers, and spoke so only I could hear. "You played well, and that Miles Davis tune was great. Will . . . will your friend be all right?"

I mumbled something that sounded vaguely affirmative, but as I followed Sol's wheelchair to the elevator, I couldn't help thinking that Annette had been zero for two: Sol wasn't exactly my friend, and he wasn't ever going to be all right.

DARKNESS

I stayed with Sol until he was in his checkered flannel old-man pj's and back in bed. With the oxygen flowing, he seemed fine, but you had to wonder what the exertion of playing had done to him. He turned to me, but didn't quite make eye contact. "*Boychik*, that wasn't a bad concert. Your friends are very talented. And you really worked hard."

How could this man get me so mad so fast? "So they're talented, and I worked hard? Thanks, Sol. You worked hard, too. I especially liked the way you tricked me into leaving my own concert, took over, and made me look like a *schlemazzel*!"

"Hey, take it easy, Alex. At least you're learning some Yiddish from me, right? And I didn't make you look like a *schlemazzel*. I just played better than you did."

"Yeah, you played better than me. That's all. Except you also never told me you played. So I made an idiot of myself for months playing in front of you. And you acted like you liked it while you were laughing in my face! Why didn't you tell me?"

"You never asked, Alex. You've been coming here since the autumn already, and you've never asked me a thing about myself. You think I was born with a hose clipped to my face?" He flicked at his nasal cannula, sighed, and continued lacing into me. "You young people never think anybody over the age of sixty ever did anything. Well, I'll tell you something, Mr. Um, Mr. Drunk Car-Crashing Hotshot: I DID PLENTY!"

He took another breath break, and I bit my lip so hard I could feel the salty blood oozing in between my front teeth. "You know Mrs. Goldfarb down the hall? She was the principal of YOUR high school for thirty-two years. Mr. Moran, in three-twenty? He ran a bank with his brother, Albert. For forty years, they built that business. Then they sold it for millions of dollars, and their kids shoved them in here three months later. Albert was dead before winter, but Mr. Moran vowed he'd outlive his no-good sons. He might just do it, too."

Sol emitted a sound that was like what you'd get if a laugh and a wheeze struck each other head-on in a freeway accident, took a sip of water from the cup on his nightstand, and started in yet again. "And you sit there counting out the hours until you can put me behind you forever. But I'll still be here, *boychik*. When I leave this place it's going to be feet first. So don't tell me I didn't tell you, I didn't tell you. Why should I have to tell you when you already know everything?"

He got quiet, sipped his water, and then lay back. He was breathing harder again, so I had a chance to yell at him for a bit while he got his wind back. But I didn't take it. "Fine, I'll ask a question: Why don't you play guitar anymore? Why did you stop?"

His eyes were closed, and he was silent for so long that I thought he must have fallen asleep. Then his lips moved, and I had to lean all the way over his bed to hear him. "Alex, Alex. I played guitar for a living. Thirty years, six nights a week. New York, Miami, California. The casinos, cruise ships, the Poconos, the Catskills. You name the room, Lou

Solomon played it. That's what they called me then, Lou Solomon. I don't know why, but my promoter thought it sounded less Jewish. Like the audience wouldn't take one look at this enormous *schnoz* on my face and figure it out anyway."

Pause, breathing, sip.

"What the hell was I talking about? Oh, the guitar. I had a wife back then. Her name was Ethel, and she was beautiful. I know, a name like Ethel maybe doesn't sound so gorgeous, but my Ethel was. She was small and bright, like a little bird. Your Laurie reminds me of her."

I interrupted, "Laurie isn't . . ."

"I'm speaking here. Do you mind? Anyway, we had a daughter, too — Judy. Cute, with a smart mouth. Always with the smart mouth. I was gone too much playing the damn guitar, but I spent enough time at home to know Judy was going to be SOMETHING someday. It was a decent life. I traveled, I met all the great ones — Monk, Dizzy, Buddy Rich, I even sat in with Miles once at the Half Note. But after a while it got old, you know what I mean?

Like lobster, maybe. You eat it once in a while, it's a delicacy. You eat it every day, soon it's just a giant bug with claws in butter sauce. And Judy was in high school, Ethel wanted to go back to work — she was a librarian — and me working nights was tough for them."

Cough, breathe, sip.

"So what happened? You retired from playing to be with your family? I think that's really . . ."

"No, I didn't retire to be with my family. I should have, but there was always one more big gig coming up, you know? So one day, Ethel drives up to Mountain Laurel, in the Poconos, to watch me play — which she didn't do that often, but Judy was sleeping at a friend's house, and maybe she was lonely. Anyway, Mountain Laurel wasn't such a great jazz room, but it was a bread-and-butter gig. Three of those in a month, and you paid the mortgage. Whatever. In the middle of the gig, I get called to the hotel phone — Judy was at the emergency room back home with a high fever. Ethel wanted me to walk off the gig to drive to the hospital with her. But I said, and it's true, 'Ethel, I've never blown a gig. Never. And people know when they book Lou Solomon, they're getting a sure thing. You go. I'm sure it'll be fine. It's only a little temperature.' We had a big argument. She said some things she maybe shouldn't have said, I said some things, too. But what was I going to do? I just couldn't walk off the gig. Ethel grabbed her purse, gave me one last look — the worst look I ever got from her — and ran out of the ballroom. The bandleader told me I should go after her, but I couldn't find her anywhere. I even sent the girl singer we had then into the ladies' room, but Ethel wasn't anywhere to be found. She must have headed straight for the car and just zoomed away. I had to go back onstage, so I did. I don't know, maybe I should have run outside or something, jumped in the band truck, and tried to catch up. But who knew what was going to happen? And Lou Solomon never blew a gig. So I went back on."

Breathe, sip, cry. Cry? Sure enough, Sol's shoulders were trembling, and tears were rolling down his cheeks. "Sol, you don't have to tell me if . . ."

"You asked, so I'm telling. It's fine. You should know this, I think. Ethel never made it home, Alex. Some drunken driver in a big truck fell asleep at the wheel on the Pennsylvania Turnpike, and knocked my Ethel's car right off the road. Right off a cliff. *Bam!* The highway patrol said she probably never even saw it coming, so at least there wasn't any pain. No pain? Ha! I never played again, until tonight. I painted houses instead. I was good at it, and I could be home at night for Judy. So she spent another couple of years at our house, and then moved away for school as soon as she could. Now I'm alone, and she's the big-shot lawyer who never even picks up her Hanukkah flowers."

I wasn't sure if this was the right move, and I'm not the most comforting guy in general, but I put my hand on Sol's arm. We stayed like that for a really, really long time, until both Sol and my left leg were fast asleep. Now I knew why Sol had gone ballistic over my little gnome episode. I pulled his blanket up to cover him, turned off the lamp over his bed, and tiptoed out of there. Just as I hit the doorway, I heard Sol turn over and mumble, "I liked 'All Blues,' kid. Keep the key."

I dozed off on the bus home, with my hand clenched tight around the key in my pocket. It had been a long day.

THE VALENTINE'S DAY MASSACRE

IN case I might have accidentally had a moment of relaxation or contentment, my high school scheduled a Sadie Hawkins dance for Valentine's Day. For those of you who haven't endured the nearly medieval torture of this particular event, a Sadie Hawkins dance is one where the girls have to ask the guys out. Now, I have very little skill in the man-woman–type area anyway, so I probably would have just stayed home in slightly depressed peace on V-day in a normal year, because the chances of my asking out a human female with any degree of success were right up there with the odds of the Chicago Cubs winning the World Series. No, worse — the Cubs winning the Super Bowl. But this Sadie Hawkins thing meant I couldn't even just give up and sulk, because at any moment some random girl might snatch me up as a partner. Granted, there wasn't exactly a waiting list to ask out semiproficient band geeks with criminal histories, but as long as there was the slightest hope, I would be sitting on pins and needles.

And of course, there was the dreaded, yet slightly exciting, prospect that Laurie might choose me. So every time I was with her I had that to add to my agony. Every day at lunch, I sat across from Laurie, choking down my oddly congealed school cafeteria pizza, watching her eat her inevitable salad, and waiting for a word from her about the dance. Of course, at least three guys would stop by the table, one by one, to talk to her, and I'd have to sweat over whether she would pop the question to them right in front of me. Seriously, I'd perspire and pray, *Not in front of me. Please, dear Lord, not right in front of me.* Then they'd leave, and I'd be vainly trying to dry off my soaked palms while awaiting the next potential suitor.

But nothing happened, nothing happened, nothing happened. It was like watching the world's greatest relief pitcher. Three up, three down. Every lunch period, three up and three down. Until one day, this girl Sarah walked up to me. Sarah was a quiet, mousy little trombone player whose most distinctive features were a massive retainer that made her sound like she was gargling marbles, and the ability to write endless pages of horrendous love poetry that she read out loud daily in our English class. Here's my impression of Sarah reading Shakespeare:

> "Womeo, ah Womeo, where faw ot dow,
> Womeo?"

Sarah reading Elizabeth Barrett Bwowning (sorry, Browning):

> "How goo I lub vee?
> Wet me cout the ways."

And here's Sarah, asking me to the Sadie Hawkins dance right in front of Laurie:

> "Hi, Wauwie. Hi, Awex. Hey, Awex, goo you what to
> go wiv me to vhe Sagie Hawkins Gance?"

I just sat there, sweating and panicking. What does one say in a situation like this? There are really no guidelines whatsoever, because this is the kind of thing that only happens to ME. After a few moments of unbearable silence — I mean, silence from me; it's not like the whole lunchroom got quiet, which is a small blessing — Laurie kicked me under the table like I was a pile of pine boards and she was really going for a trophy. I wasn't sure what she meant to convey, other than a painful bruise, but she succeeded in prodding me into action. "Sure, Sarah, I'd be glad to."

While Sarah and I were working out the details, and I was trying to rub my shin without being too pathetically obvious, Laurie somehow left the cafeteria. By the time I said a fond farewell to my new hot date and hobbled out into the hall, Laurie was long gone.

While I was making these swell plans, my parents were getting their own warped ideas for the upcoming holiday. They were in "couples therapy" together, because, as Dad put it, "We want to start fresh, and not make the same mistakes again that we made last time." They could have saved seventy-five bucks an hour if they had just come to me instead. It was no big mystery: I would have just told Dad to stop getting it on with my teachers. But anyway, their therapist had this great idea that they should try to have a big, ceremonial, perfect "first date" on Valentine's Day. So they had a whole elaborate scenario worked out, with fancy clothes, flowers, dinner, dancing, and God knew what else. Every time I went to Dad's (which I was grudgingly doing maybe twice a week now), he would try to get me to tell him what Mom was going to wear. Then I'd get home, and Mom would interrogate me about Dad's wardrobe choice for the evening. Like a) I cared, and, b) I paid attention to the weird sounds that came out when their lips were moving. I hoped things would go well for them, or at least I mostly did, but I wanted nothing to do with any of it, because even if they were forgetting, I remembered how peachy their romance had turned out to be the first time around. Whatever, it was just another interesting V-day plot twist.

The day after my first disastrous lunch with Laurie, I was treated to the pleasure of another. I lurched over to the table with an exaggerated limp so Laurie would know she had probably hobbled me for life with her vicious kick, and said, "Hi. Salad today? A bold choice."

She fired right back, "Verbally challenged band-geek date? A bold choice."

"What's your problem? She came over. She asked me out. When I didn't immediately jump up and start kissing her instantly, you kicked me under the table. So I said yes, just like you wanted me to."

"I didn't want you to say yes, I wanted you to say no."

"Gee, too bad you didn't give me the ankle-kicking Morse code translation kit so I could figure that out. I guess I'm a little rusty on distinguishing the yes kick from the no kick. And why did you want me to say no?"

"Well, because you don't *like* Sarah. At least, you've never mentioned her before. It just seems kind of cruel to lead her on. She's obviously been longing for you in her heart, pining away, her tragic tears dripping down her face and rusting her adorable little retainer."

"Oh, *I'm* cruel? You're busting on her orthodontic issues, but I'm the cruel one? And what if I had said no? Then I would have sat at home, miserable, and she would have, too."

Laurie chewed her lip for a moment. "Alex, you weren't going to be sitting home on Valentine's Day."

"What do you mean?"

"Well, I kind of thought . . ."

Before she could finish, a huge shadow fell over us. We both looked up at the tanklike form of Brad Hunter, the star offensive lineman on our football team. Like a heavily armored attack vehicle, he towered above the table with an air of menace. Unlike a heavily armored attack vehicle, he started talking to Laurie. "Listen, Laurie, I know this is supposed to be a girls-asking-guys thing, but I think you're really special, and I'd like to take you to the dance. I mean, if you don't have other plans."

Laurie gave me yet another of her deadly and accurate kicks, and smiled sweetly at Brad. "No, I don't have any other plans."

Women! Can't live with 'em, can't walk.

• • •

The night of the dance, I was all set to make the most of the situation. My mom had graciously un-grounded me, perhaps so she could be home alone when my dad arrived to pick her up. I had on a nice pair of black pants and a dark green sweater that Laurie had bought me because she said it "set off my eyes." I had shaved, which, okay, maybe I didn't tech-nically have a massive growth of facial hair, but hey! It allowed me to feel entitled to splash on some after-shave. I had brushed my teeth — twice — and rinsed with mouthwash until my mouth was a veritable gar-den of minty freshness. I had combed my hair so it didn't quite have the usual "brown Q-Tip" thing happening. I was just about to set out on the short walk to Sarah's house, which was only a block from school, when the phone rang.

My mom jumped about seven feet sideways and almost yanked the phone out of the wall — not that she was tense or anything, right? I only heard her end of the convo, obviously, but it didn't have a good ring to it:

"Hello. This is she. He WHAT? He can't? When did this happen? Where is he? He asked for . . . ? Okay, I'll see what I can do. Thank you."

She turned to me. I was all ready to hear my dad had suddenly fled the country with my gym teacher or something, but I've never had a big gift for premonition. "Alex, I have some bad news. Mr. Lewis . . . Sol . . . is in the hospital. He has pneumonia. I know the timing is bad , but he asked to see you."

Oh, crud. "All right, I'll go tomorrow morning. Can I skip school?"

"Alex, you don't get it. Sol has pneumonia. Pneumonia kills people, especially old people.

Especially old people with emphysema. He might not be . . . around . . . tomorrow morning."

I thought fast. "Mom, can you drive me right now? We'll have to stop at Sarah's house to tell her what's going on."

Mom sighed. This wasn't exactly the vision she had had for this evening. "Okay, get your coat. I'll call your father from the car."

At Sarah's, I ran up and rang the bell. I'd been expecting her mom or dad to answer the door so we could have one of those awkward predate Spanish Inquisition rituals, but Sarah must have beaten them to it. She looked really, really pretty. I'd never seen her in anything except jeans and T-shirts before, but she was wearing some kind of silky green dress thing that suited her, somehow. Her eyes were green like mine, which had never registered with me before. Something else was different, too, but it didn't click for me until she shouted, "Bye, Mom. Bye, Dad. I'll be back by midnight. I have my cell if you need me!"

When she smiled shyly at me, I had visual confirmation: The retainer had been deep-sixed for the night. Sarah could speak! So now I had a date who had basically transformed herself into a princess, but our gala ball had turned into a bedside vigil. I had to 'fess up to the facts, so on the way back to the car, I stopped walking and gave her the update. "Sarah, I have some bad news. I volunteer at the nursing home . . ."

"For that old man, Sol, right? I know all about it — you got in trouble for drunk driving, and then you got sentenced to work at the nursing home. But then you really bonded with this old guy, and you put on a concert with Steven and Annette, and your guy played guitar, right? I think it's heroic the way you're helping an old man in need!"

How did she know all this? I had to ask. "How do you know all this?"

"Didn't Bryan Gilson tell you? He told me all about you. I mean, I knew you from jazz band, and I knew you were cute. . . ." God, my mom must have been smirking if she was hearing this through the open car window. "But Bryan was the one who told me how deep and sensitive you are. And then I wasn't going to ask you out anyway, because of your — you know — relationship with Laurie, but Bryan said it was okay, and that Laurie was going with one of his jock friends anyway. So here we are, and I'm glad. I'm sorry, you were saying?"

"Um, well, it's like this: Sol — the old man — is in the hospital. I just got the call, and he's really sick. He asked for me, and this might be, like, his deathbed. So I have to go right now to see him. You can come, if you want. Or my mom can probably drop you off at the dance, and I could meet you there after . . ."

Sarah stopped me with a hand on my forearm. Her hand was warm and dry. And she was looking at me with weird googly eyes. "Alex, I'd be honored to go visit your friend with you. Let's go there."

So we jumped in the car, and that's what we did. When Mom dropped us off, I told her to go ahead with her date. She gave me a twenty and told me to call a cab when we were ready to go from the hospital to the dance. As we walked up to the hospital's information desk, Sarah grabbed my hand and squeezed it. This was a weird night for sure. And I couldn't decide whether I should thank Bryan or kill him.

Sol's room upstairs was "semiprivate," which is hospital code for "not private." So there was a guy in the bed by the window all hooked up to tubes and wires. Sol was by the door, propped partway up on pillows, with two different IV bags dripping into his arm and a cannula clipped between his nostrils. His glasses weren't on, which made his nose look both bigger and sunken at the same time. His lips were blue.

God, his lips were blue. I'm no doctor, and the ninety-one I got in biology freshman year probably didn't qualify me as a diagnostic expert, but I was fairly certain blue lips were not one of the top ten signs of robust health. I said hello, and he turned toward my voice.

"Alex, *boychik*, is that you? I knew you'd come." His voice sounded like he was trying to speak through a mouthful of coffee grounds. BOILING coffee grounds. I went right over and put my hand on his shoulder — his blue, IV-punctured hand was just a little too scary for me. While he was catching his breath after this long speech, Sarah stepped up next to me.

"Sol, this is . . ."

"I know who this is. What, I get a little cough and take off my glasses and you think I'm suddenly a complete *schmeggege*? It's wonderful to see you again, Laurie."

Uh-oh. Sarah stiffened and pulled her hand away.

Sol grabbed her hand. "Let me have a good look at you, dear." For what seemed like maybe the length of — oh, I don't know — a year on Pluto, he squinted up at her and breathed raggedly. "Alex, va-va-voom! She's all dressed up tonight. So where is your husband taking you this evening, Mrs. Um?"

She didn't know how to reply to that, and neither did I, but Sol seemed to catch the look that passed between us. "Oh, I know, I know. You aren't married YET. But I might die tomorrow, so I'm using the present tense — HOO-hah, excuse me — for the future."

"Sol, uh, she isn't . . ."

"Oh, I know. She isn't comfortable talking out loud about this, are you, Laurie, honey? Don't worry, then — we all understand exactly what's going on here, right?"

Sarah's eyes were flashing danger signals at this point, but I couldn't work out a way to stop Sol from digging the hole even deeper. You had to give me credit for trying, though. "Sol, listen to me. This isn't . . ."

"Oh, I don't think it's the end for me either. You don't have to try to cheer me up, Alex. And there's no need for crying, Laurie. I'll pull through fine. These doctors are excellent. And I think this one nurse likes me. She winked at me before. I told her I was too old for her, but these women just can't resist a man with his *tuchis* hanging out — sorry, Laurie — with his *tuchis* hanging out of a robe like this."

I gave up on my attempts to correct Sol, which meant that Sarah sulked and fumed through the rest of the visit. Sol and I talked for maybe fifteen minutes more, and then a nurse came in and told us that visiting hours were over. As soon as we stood up to go, Sol launched into the longest, deepest coughing fit I'd ever heard. I mean, even for him, this was something special. There was harrumph-ing, and HOO-hah-ing, and barking, then more of all three. When he suddenly grabbed a cup from the night-stand and spat into it, he got his wind back for a second. He said to Sarah, "Laurie, sweetie, can you please get me a glass of water from the nurses' station? I appear to have schmutzed into my drinking cup."

When she cleared the doorway, I saw my chance: "Sol, that's not Laurie. Her name is Sarah. She's a trombone player in my school jazz band, and she's my date for a dance tonight."

He gave me such a deadpan look that I wanted to shake him. "Of course, she's not Laurie. Do you think pneumonia makes a man blind? What school do you go to again?"

"Well, I mean, you said . . . she isn't . . . you're not wearing your glasses, so I thought . . ."

"*Boychik*, haven't you ever heard of contact lenses? You really need to get with the times here."

"Then you knew this whole . . . ?"

Sol's malicious, yet radiant, smile told me everything I needed to know: "GOTCHA!"

Sarah came in with the water at that point, just as Sol doubled over in another spasm of coughing. But it sounded to me like there might have been just a touch of laughter mixed in. I apologized profusely to Sarah all the way downstairs, and while we waited outside for our cab, AND on the whole ride over. AND as we headed into the dance. She kept telling me over and over that it was no problem, she understood, yada yada. But it didn't take a genius to realize Sol had a better chance of running off to Aruba with his nurse than I did of getting anywhere with Sarah.

And the odds didn't get any better inside. The first people we ran into on our way to the dance floor were Laurie and her monolithic side of beef, Brad. She was wearing — and I couldn't believe my eyes — a fire-engine–red dress that fit her like the designer had run out of fabric in the middle and switched over to spray paint to finish the job. Brad was sporting baggy slate-colored pants, a slate-colored shirt, and a slate-colored sweater. I don't want to insult the guy, but all I'm saying is this: If you had been mugged by an African water animal, and the safari police placed Brad in a lineup with four rhinos, it would have been pretty hard to disqualify him as a suspect.

He was almost incomprehensibly bigger than she was. Approaching them from a distance, the view reminded me of a picture book I used to love when I was around five, called *The Little Red Lighthouse and the Great Gray Bridge*. But this story was a lot less entertaining for me. And when we got close enough that I started worrying we might get caught up and sucked into Brad's gravitational field, we had to actually communicate.

"Hi, Laurie. Hi, Brad."

"Hi, Alex. Hey, Sarah. *You're* fashionably late."

(Yeah, and your partner is fashionably rectangular. So?)

"Well, we ran into a little obstacle."

Brad's nearly subsonic voice lumbered into the fray. "Oh, like a lawn gnome, maybe?"

I thought, *Wow, we ARE really late. Laurie had time to teach Brad to SPEAK!* But I didn't say it, because I'm above that sort of thing. Oh, and because Brad could basically reach out one granitelike finger and smear me into a thin paste. So I just chuckled. "Good one, Brad. No, actually we had to stop at the hospital on the way over."

I stopped and waited for that to sink in. While Brad was probably still struggling to cope with my daunting use of a three-syllable word, Laurie asked, "The hospital? Why? What's going on?"

"Uh, Sol has pneumonia."

"Oh, my God! How is he? Can he speak? Is he coherent? I have to go see him."

Sarah saw her opening. "Don't worry, Laurie. He thinks you already did!"

Laurie raised an eyebrow, and reached out to grab my arm. Sarah was probably about ready to reach into her bag and spray me with Mace, and it might have been my imagination, but I think Brad was actually RUMBLING at me. Laurie said, in that totally characteristic, I-don't-care-what-anybody-else-thinks way, "Alex, take me to the hospital!"

Who knew that three people from such different backgrounds, and with such varied emotional needs and perspectives, could all say, "BUT . . ." at exactly the same instant?

"No buts. I'm sorry, but this is a life on the line, not some cheesy high school theme dance. Look, Sarah, was your date with Alex going well?"

"Uhh . . ."

"My point exactly. And Brad? Do you feel we've made an immortal, transcendent soul-to-soul connection tonight?"

"Huh?"

"See? Brad, meet Sarah. Sarah's a very talented musician. And Sarah, meet Brad. Brad does the most amazing impression of a Himalaya! Alex, get your coat back on and let's blow this Popsicle stand."

Twenty minutes later, we were sneaking up to Sol's floor on a service elevator. A nurse busted us, but Laurie did this whole Oscar-winning performance as Sol's frantic granddaughter, and she granted us a small exemption from the visiting-hours rules. There are times when I have to admit Laurie is very nearly a superhero of some sort, although it would have been tricky for her to conceal a costume under the particular dress she was wearing. Sol noticed the outfit right off the bat. "Laurie, it's wonderful to see you again so soon. You changed your dress. This one is a lot nicer. I hope Alex told you that."

I blushed and bit my lip.

Laurie went through a big Q&A about Sol's whole health situation while I tried not to check out her whole skintight-dress situation. He assured her that he was fine, and his color definitely DID look better than it had even an hour and a half before. Then he asked Laurie if he could speak to me for a moment alone, man to man. She raised the old eyebrow, but kissed him good-bye without a peep of protest and walked out into the hall. Sol patted the edge of his bed, and I sat there. "*Boychik*," he intoned in a manly-man-giving-another-manly-man-advice voice, "That's the girl for you. *That's* your dance partner, not some tuba-honking mouse."

"Sol, Sarah plays the trombone."

"Whatever, do what you want. Go, date your little Sousaphone player. I'm old, what do I know? But when you're done messing around, I hope Laurie is still going to be waiting for you. From the look of her in that red dress, I wouldn't count on it."

It had been an odd day, so maybe my guard was down more than usual. "Sol, I wouldn't mind going out with Laurie. But SHE doesn't notice ME that way."

"Alex, you really are a *meshuggener* sometimes. This girl follows you around, she worries about you all the time, she even plays nicely with your grumpy old friend Sol. She notices you, all right. And she notices you noticing her. You just don't notice her noticing you. Oy, this is giving me a headache. But the point is, time is precious, and a girl like that is precious. Now stop wasting both of them and let me get some sleep. On second thought, maybe call that beautiful nurse in here and see if it's time for my next dose of cough medicine. I love that stuff!"

As Laurie and I left, Sol had another huge paroxysm of coughing. It was almost as if he had been putting the cough aside in order to concentrate on his advice to me. And when Laurie leaned her head on my shoulder in the elevator, I was really hoping the advice had been right. "Where should we go now?" she asked me. "I don't think Sarah and Brad will be so excited to see us back at the dance, do you?"

"No, and I'd rather be with you tonight. I mean, all the time. I mean . . ."

She put a finger to my lips and I noticed that her short, bitten-down fingernails were polished red to match the outfit. "Shh," she whispered, and tilted her head up to me. Did she want me to kiss her? How weird was this going to be? Should it be like a real kiss, with passion and stuff? Or more of an experimental, pecking kind of deal? And why did this elevator smell like month-old cabbage?

Putting aside my deep thoughts, I made my move. Suavely, with one deft motion, I reached behind her and pushed the red STOP button on the elevator's control panel. And an alarm started blaring at a bone-shattering volume. Laurie jerked up off my shoulder so fast that we banged teeth. As I slapped frantically at the controls to pull the button back out, Laurie started cracking up. My blushing reflex was sure getting a whole lot of practice for one day. When I got the button released, there was a shocking silence. Laurie reined in her guffaws, and was just sort of letting off a random giggle every couple of seconds as she stared at my lip. "Alex, you're bleeding! Let me — GIGGLE — help you." She fished a dubious-looking tissue out of her purse and dabbed at my face. She leaned closer to get a better look, and it was almost starting to look like Round Two, when we reached the ground floor. The doors opened onto a packed lobby, with two aging security guards right in front.

"Everything okay, kids? We heard the alarm."

"Yes, sorry, sir. I just . . . uh . . . needed to stop the car for a second. Because . . ."

"Yeah, I can see the 'because' with my own two

eyes, son. Hey, aren't you the kid with the lawn gnome?"

"Uh, Sarge? Is that you?"

He gave me a long glare, which relaxed into a grin. "Yeah, I moonlight here — hey, I got two daughters in college. You're looking a little better than the last couple of times I saw you. I asked your judge, and she said you're keeping your nose clean. Anyway, you'd best be moving on now — and stay out of trouble."

Laurie and I walked through the crowd, as Sarge's partner said, "Wow, did you see the way she looked at him? If that boy stays out of trouble tonight, it'll be a miracle."

GOOD MORNING, WORLD!

The day after the dance was interesting. Because V-day had fallen on a Sunday, and our school's Student Council was a bunch of idiots, the dance had been held on the actual evening of the fourteenth, and we were all staggeringly tired at school on Monday morning. When I collapsed into my home-room seat, all I wanted was to slump there and pray the gigantic cappuccino thing I'd guzzled en route would start waking me up soon. But Bryan Gilson must have had a quicker metabolism, because he was totally alert and all ready to gloat. "So did you have fun with Sarah last night? You owe me one, buddy. Somebody had to get tired of watching you drool all over yourself in front of Laurie every day and get you a woman. And somebody had to spare Laurie the inconvenience of denying your sorry booty if you finally ever got the courage to be a man and ask her out. So I got my boy Bradley to help her out, too. And now you and the ninja master can settle down and be normal friends, right?"

Laurie walked in, sort of sashayed and glided her way past Bryan, and leaned over me. She put her arms around my neck from behind and kissed the top of my head. "Mmm," she purred. "You smell like French vanilla. How was your very short sleep, sweetheart?"

NOW I was awake. Considering that nothing had happened after the hospital except one of our usual three-hour frozen talks on my front porch while we were on a stakeout for my mom's return, this was news to me. But even though Bryan couldn't see Laurie's battle-hardened fingers digging into my abdomen, I could feel them. And for once I actually got the hint. "Great, honey. I was dreaming about you all — night — long."

"Mmmm . . . that wasn't a dream, sweet boy. It was a telepathic promise."

Did you ever play Ping-Pong in front of a cat? They sit right down as close to the net as they can, and watch in astonishment as the ball pings and

pongs back and forth. And they look rather aston-
ished every time a new volley starts, like it is just an
almost unbearable source of wonderment that this
hollow plastic sphere is flying in a pattern before
their very eyes AGAIN. Well, that was basically the
vibe Bryan was giving off as he tried to make sense
of this exchange.

The bell rang for the end of homeroom, and
Laurie squeezed my bicep, bumped me with her hip,
winked, and slipped around Bryan out the door. He
and I walked out into the hall together, with him
squawking little sounds like, "Wha-huh? Umm-urk.
Lau-you-I-huh? Ugg."

I said, "Yup, you really did fix me up. Thanks,
bud. By the way, I think it's great that you're now
relaxed enough around me to reveal your inner
caveman."

And then the shadow fell. Brad! Astonishing. He
actually dwarfed Bryan. In case I'd been wondering
what astronauts feel like when they come around
the dark side of the moon, and see the Earth taking
up the entire sky, now I knew. His hand fell on my

shoulder, and if my knees hadn't already been weak from Laurie's advances, they sure were wobbly under his massive body force. His tremendous head was mere inches from mine. And there was this twisted grimace on his face. "Hey, Gregory!"

Whoa, I thought, *here comes the killing part of my morning.*

But then a strange realization came over me: The contorted expression was what happened when a football lineman attempted to smile. He thundered, "Thanks!" And I noticed that crunched in under his other redwoodlike arm was a petite little shape with brown hair on top.

The voice of Brad's new girlfriend reverberated from his right armpit: "Yeah, Awex. Fanks!"

Walking home from school that afternoon, Laurie was in an exuberant mood. "Did you see how I got Bryan going? He really thinks we hooked up last night!"

Of course, her act had been so good that I, myself, had been halfway caught between wanting that, and believing it. But if she could be casual, I could be casual-er. More casual. Whatever. "Yeah, we're a great team. We should be secret agents. You could be the deadly martial-arts assassin . . ."

"Great! I love those slinky black Kevlar outfits they wear."

"Yeah, me, too. And I could be the . . . uh . . ."

"Slightly deranged ex-convict? Elevator saboteur? Drunken getaway driver? Lawn Gnome Terminator?"

Really, with a life as entertaining as mine, who needs caffeine?

February 16

Dear Judge Trent,

I just realized that I never wrote to fill you in on the results of the big concert at the home. All of the attendees had a wonderful time, and several people commented on the excellent guitar playing.

Not my guitar playing, though. The big surprise of the night was that my friend Solomon Lewis used to be a professional guitarist. Evidently, he swore off playing many years ago because he blames himself for a drunk-driving accident in which his wife died.

It's really sad, and I am starting to understand why Mr. Lewis is sometimes rather bitter. He has a grown-up daughter who is a lawyer somewhere, and she doesn't speak to him. It's pretty horrible, really, because he wasn't even in the car with his wife when she crashed, but somehow the fault falls on him anyway.

I guess I would be snappish, too, in Mr. Lewis's place.

Anyway, we gave Mr. Lewis a chance to play at the concert. I felt great that he got an opportunity to entertain people in such a positive way, especially because now he is in the hospital with pneumonia. This may have been his last chance to play the guitar for an audience, and I am proud to have provided it for him.

Sincerely,

Alex Gregory

February 19

Dear Alex,

I am glad your event went well. What you have discovered about your client's tragic past is very interesting. Perhaps, given the nature of your offense, you were deliberately assigned to Mr. Lewis so that you could learn some lessons together.

That is, after all, the point of the Full Circle program.

Do keep up the good work, and continue to keep me informed of your progress.

Sincerely,

Judge J. Trent

THE MISSION

Later that week, Sol pitched a plan to help me out. He was back at the home, and was having a post-pneumonia burst of energy. "Hey, Alex, you haven't played guitar for me in a while."

"Well, Sol, don't hold your breath. I can't play in front of you now that you blew me off the stage. It would just be stupid."

"Stupid, schmupid. What's stupid is to quit when you have a good thing going."

"I'm not quitting, I'm just not playing here. And besides, I don't have a good thing going. I have a mediocre thing going. *You* had a good thing going. And come to think of it, *you* quit."

"For this, I came back from the hospital? *Boychik*, I'm not trying to fight with you here. I'm trying to help you out, to make you an offer, to give your life a meaning and a purpose. So you don't just stumble around like a *schmegegge* all the time, drinking too much, stealing cars, and who knows what other hooligan foolishness."

"Wow, I'm glad you're not trying to fight. But where's the help part?"

"Here's the help part, Mister Smart Aleck. Next time you come, you bring your guitar here, and I'll teach you some things you need to know. Then you'll practice them and come back for another lesson. I figure if you really set your mind to it, and don't get all distracted chasing around everything in a red dress, you'll be ready for your next concert in six weeks."

"What next concert?"

"Well, the one I set up in April."

"April? I don't even know whether the other musicians are available in April."

"You mean, Steven and Annette? You just missed them the other day. They visited when you left, and we picked a date for you to play again. And not to compare you to anybody, but Annette brought a lovely fruitcake. You brought me *bupkes*."

"I don't believe you, Sol!"

"What? It's true. When was the last time you brought me a little snack? I don't expect much, but some baked goods once in a while would be a nice gesture."

"Not about the fruitcake. I can't believe you set this up without asking me."

"I'm asking, I'm asking. Of course, I'm asking for maybe some cookies next time you come, too, but what are my chances?"

"You're not asking me, you're telling me. And the answer is no. I don't want to be embarrassed again."

"You know what, Mr. Sensitive? When I was coming up, if a guy got shown up on the bandstand, he woodshedded. He went back home and practiced. Then he practiced. Then he practiced some more. Then he got back up onstage and — maybe, just maybe — he was ready the second time around. So what are you going to do, cry in a corner forever, or be a man and take some free guitar lessons?"

"I'll tell you what, Sol: I'll play the concert. . . ."

A smile began its slow spread across his wrinkled cheeks.

". . . as long as you play it with me. So how about it, Mr. Jump Back in the Saddle? Are you with me?"

Sol thought it over through the course of a moderately gross coughing fit. After he spat, drank, and took a few really slow breaths, I got my response. "I'll tell YOU what, *boychik*. I'll see you in two days. Bring a guitar, some sheet music, maybe some blank paper. And would it kill you to stop and pick up a Danish or two?"

• • •

At home, I found my dad in the kitchen, wearing an apron and cooking for my mom. I asked whether he was officially moving back in, and he smiled. "I don't know, bud. You know we're trying to go slow and easy with this, but I almost think it might be time to try being under one roof again. Here, try this."

"What is it?"

"Alfredo. It's a creamy cheese sauce."

"Since when do you know how to make

ANYTHING, much less a so-called 'creamy cheese sauce'?"

"Oh, Alex. Gimme a break. People can change, right? Now, taste it already."

"I don't know, Dad. I've been burned before."

"Hmm, is that a resentful little metaphor?"

"No, it's a statement about something that sometimes happens to the roof of my mouth when I consume hot foods." I took a wincing little mini-sip off of the wooden spoon my dad was holding out to me. "Hey, not bad. Maybe an old dog can learn new tricks."

"Or at least new recipes. I'll just add a little more Parmesan, turn up the heat a bit, and . . ."

Just then we heard a big clattering crash upstairs, followed by a piercing screech from my mom. I charged up the steps right behind my father, who was still holding the spoon in his right hand. He was ready for action, in a chef-style kind of way. "What is it, Janet?"

She was standing over a shattered picture frame, sucking her thumb. "Oh, Simon, look at this! I was trying to hang our wedding portrait back up; I thought it was time. But I banged my finger with the hammer, and dropped everything. The frame is broken, and the picture is probably scratched up. I'm afraid to move. Can you look?"

Dad handed the spoon off to me, got down on his hands and knees, and crawled through the chaos of shattered glass. The picture was flipped upside down, and was resting against my mom's bare foot. Dad gingerly lifted it off, and I saw that the actual photo looked fine — but something had cut the top of my mother's foot pretty hideously. Since Mom is a nurse, once there was a bloody wound she took control right away. "Simon, pick me up. No, under the arms. Now carry me to the bed. Alex, don't just stand there — go get the vacuum and a garbage can, and start picking up the broken glass. All right, Simon, watch out for the bedspread. We'll need — uh — two towels and some gauze."

While Dad and I scrambled around like we were on an Easter-egg hunt, Mom sat hunched over on the bed and pressed a wad of tissues to the gushing slit in her foot. "This is going to need stitches. Oh, Simon. I'm sorry. I broke our portrait and ruined your big dinner plans."

He rushed back into the room and gently — oh, so gently — wrapped her foot in gauze. "It's okay, Janet. Broken things can be fixed. And I'm glad I'm here for you."

Oh, how freaking romantic. Gory, yet freaking romantic.

Three minutes later, Apron Man and Gimp Lady were on the way to the hospital. I realized I was hungry, and walked into the kitchen. That's when I noticed the bitter smell. And when I lifted the lid of Dad's creation, I got a face full of acrid brown smoke. The sauce was now a thin wafer of charred carbon.

Here was a lesson I could tell the judge I'd learned: Some people get the romance, and some people get coal for dinner.

THE SAINTS GO
MARCHIN' IN

"**No,** no, Alex! Jazz has to have a swing to it. All the time, a swing."

"But this is a sad song."

"All the more reason it should swing, then. Listen: Do you know how jazz started out? As funeral music. In New Orleans, when somebody would die, they would all walk down to the cemetery with a band playing sad songs. But on the way BACK from the cemetery, they danced. The band played fast, they played happy. And the people danced. Even in sorrow, jazz should sound like there's dancing in it. Have you ever heard 'When the Saints Go Marching In?'"

"Uh, I'm not sure."

Sol held out his hands for my guitar, and I handed it over. I was ready for a break anyway. It was our first day of official practice, and he had shown me some new scale patterns first. After I had played those for maybe twenty minutes, he'd shown me some finger exercises, some new chords, and now a brand-new song. My fingers felt like they were going to shrivel up and die, and apparently, I hadn't done anything right yet.

He took the guitar and played a simple little melody. First he played just the melody, with no bounce to it at all, like this:

Ding-ding-ding-ding.

It was the corniest thing I had ever heard. Like, if Mister Rogers had played guitar, this would have been his big solo feature. Then Sol played just the melody again, with a swing:

Ding-a-ding-a-ding-ding.

This was starting to sound a little hipper. Next, he played the chords on the low strings, and the melody on the high strings, all at the same time. Suddenly, it was so bouncy I couldn't sit still. When he played it again, and added a call-and-response part, I found myself tapping along on my legs and smiling:

Dinga-dinga-ding-ding.   (Dinga-dinga-ding-ding.)

Finally, he played the chords, but sang the words to the tune AND answered them with the response part on the high strings:

"Oh, when the saints   (dinga-dinga-ding-ding.)
Go marching in   (dinga-dinga-ding-ding.)
Oh, when the saints go marching in,
(deet-deet-deet-dooby-doo-wah)
Oh how I want to be in that number,
when the saints go marchin' in."

When he stopped, he was wildly out of breath. Claudelle was standing in the doorway clapping, but he was too wrapped up in catching up on oxygen to notice. She said to me, under her breath, "He sounds good. But that's goin' to get harder and harder for him now. You watch. You'd better be careful not to push him too hard, or he's goin' to *be* in that number soon enough."

On the way to my third or fourth lesson, I realized something that should have probably hit me much sooner: We had one guitar, and two guitarists. How were we both going to play at this concert? I came up with a plan, and told Sol about it right away. "Hey, Sol, listen. We have a little problem, but I think I have it all figured out."

"YOU have it all figured out? THIS I've got to hear."

"Ha-ha. Look, we've got two of us, but only one guitar. I have a feeling that will add a bit too much challenge to the duet portion of the concert program."

"So I won't play. That's fine, *boychik*. I've been pretty tired lately anyway." Which he had.

"No, you'll play. Here's the thing: My hundred hours of mandated public service are almost up.

After that, I'll get to keep the five bucks an hour I earn for being here. I was planning to use that money to save up for a car, but we all know that, thanks to my brilliance, I have a few years to do that anyway. So I have a schedule I just made, and if I can get Annette and Steven to practice here sometimes, I think I can make about three hundred bucks in the next few weeks. Then I'll buy a cheap jazz guitar used somewhere. I can play that, and you can have my Telecaster. And, um, you don't have to pay me back or anything. Consider it payment for these amazing lessons. I've never improved this fast in my life."

"Wait a minute, Mr. Um. You're telling me you'd play a used, old, dusty guitar and let me use your beautiful Telecaster? Are you really sure?"

"Sol, I'm sure. Why?"

"Wait, wait. Are you SURE you're sure? You'll play the old thing, I'll play the Tele, and you're even willing to pay the bill?"

"YES, that's what I'm saying."

"Hmmm. Do you still have the key I gave you?"

"Yeah, it's on my key chain." I took it out. "See?"

"Okay, Alex, it's time for my breathing treatment. Why don't you take a walk down to the storage lockers at the end of the hall? That key fits my locker, number three-forty-four. Just like the room number. Anyway, bring me what you find."

"Is there only one thing in there, or will I know what I'm looking for?"

As the respiratory therapy guy strapped the little mask on his head, Sol said, "You'll know, *boychik*. Believe me, you'll know."

I took my walk then. Down the hall, around the corner, chat with the nurses, buy a candy bar, hang out with Mrs. Goldfarb. Killing time, because I was kinda nervous to see what was in the locker. But when I saw the respiratory therapist leave Sol's room, I figured that was my cue. I walked down the long hall to the locker, not knowing what would be in there. A jug of water, rigged to dump on my head? A spring-loaded pie-throwing device? I definitely felt a "GOTCHA" coming on, but Sol hadn't had quite the usual gloating smirk on his face. I shoved the key in the lock, took a deep breath, and turned it. The mechanism was creaky; I could tell nobody had been in the locker for a long time. Okay, that meant the pie-thrower was probably not a realistic threat, anyway. When I opened the door, there wasn't much to see, just a few big boxes, labeled RECORD COLLECTION, FAMILY PHOTOS, MUSIC PHOTOS, and JUDY. But when I pushed the top box aside a bit, I saw a black shape sticking up from behind the pile, a shape I knew. It was a very, very dusty guitar case. Choking on the dust, I pulled it up and over the boxes, then straightened the pile back up. As I closed the locker and headed back to Sol's room, I was dying to see what was inside. I was also dying of a sudden allergy fit, so I stopped by the nurses' desk and rubbed down the outside of the case with a cleaning wipe Juanita gave me. I figured the big surprise wouldn't be quite right if Sol keeled over and died from the dust.

Sol was sitting up in bed in the usual position, but his posture was different somehow. He looked taller, straighter, more alert. And I realized that the guitar in this case was something he really wanted to see again. I set it on the bed, with the latches facing him. He spun it around toward me. "You open it, *boychik.* I already know what's in there."

Click. One latch. *Click,* the second. *Click,* number three. I tried to swing the lid up. Doh! This was one of the old-fashioned kind of cases that has the extra latch by the bottom. *Click.* Deep breath for me. Shallow breath for Sol. Slowly, I started to lift that lid again. I sort of squinched my eyes up so I wouldn't see too much too soon, but I knew I was looking at a special instrument. The body was a gleaming blond wood, with cream-colored binding around the edges and F-holes. The hardware was gold, with one of those fancy harp tailpieces you see on guitars in old, old movies. The neck was, literally, a work of art, with gorgeous slanted, parallel blocks of pearl inlay at the first, third, fifth, and seventh frets. The headstock of the guitar had the word "D'Angelico" in beautiful, flowing script, over an elaborate art-deco design. And inlaid into the twelfth fret in gleaming mother-of-pearl was a single word: GOTCHA!

My voice was shaky. "Sol, is this what I think it is?"

"What am I, a mind reader? If you're thinking it's a toaster, you're wrong. However, if you're thinking it's a very valuable 1954 D'Angelico New Yorker archtop with a custom inlay, you're smarter than you look."

"And I'm supposed to PLAY this?"

"Alex, it's yours. You could strap it to your feet and use it for skiing if you want to, but I personally think that would be wasteful."

"Why me?"

"You gave me your Telecaster, and you can't go up onstage next month and play the washboard. So now you have a real jazz guitar."

"But I'm not a real jazz guitar player."

"So you'll grow into it. Or you'll wait until I die, sell it, and pay for two years of college. Whatever. Now, tune that thing up and let's play."

Holy cow, holy cow, holy . . . freaking . . . COW!

My hands were starting to tremble, but I picked up the D'Angelico, sat in the big chair, and tuned it (the guitar, not the chair). Even with decades-old strings, the thing sounded like a heavenly choir of angels. Well, all right, a heavenly choir of tone-deaf angels — at least until I finished tuning. When everything sounded good, I played a few chords. Then I played a few more chords. Then a single-note run. Then some of the call-and-response chord-melody stuff Sol had been showing me. I looked up, and Sol was grinning from ear to ear, but his eyes were watery, too. He growled, "Nice-sounding hunk of wood, eh? Think you can work with it?"

"It'll have to do, I suppose."

"Good. Now let's see how you're doing with the chord-substitution exercises from last time. And remember to keep your right wrist loose. If you lose the swing, it doesn't matter if you're playing a solid-gold guitar with diamond inlays — nobody's going to be happy. All right, then. One-two-three-four!"

THE WORK OF BREATHING

The next time I went to visit Sol, I was bearing gifts, but he wasn't in the room. Leonora was walking by, and came over to me. "Hello, Alex. I haven't seen you in a while, but I hear you and Mr. Lewis have been exchanging instruments. If someone had told me three months ago that I'd see the day when Sol started sharing his things with others, I wouldn't have believed it. You and he have quite a special relationship, young man. My hat's off to you."

"Thank you. Uh, where is he?"

"Just at the doctor's for some tests. You know, it's becoming more difficult to manage his CHF, so the medical folks here have been consulting a lot with the cardiologists over at the hospital."

"CHF?"

"Congestive heart failure. He is doing remarkably well for a man with so little remaining lung capacity, but after all, his emphysema is terminal."

I had a lump in my throat all of a sudden, like someone had snuck down in there with a chicken bone, some crazy glue, and a bad grudge. "Yes, I know he's in bad shape. Will . . . when . . . when will he be coming back?"

"You have about an hour or so, at the least. Why don't you go on into his room and play your guitar for a while? That way, you will be ready to impress him when he arrives. Oh, he so enjoys your time together."

"Sure. Thank you, Leonora." She strode off to depress somebody else, and I walked down to Sol's locker to get the guitar — I still couldn't even begin to think of it as MY guitar. I reached in for the handle of the case and missed. The boxes tipped, tumbled, and crashed, although I made a spectacular diving save and grabbed the guitar case before it had a chance to hit the ground. Then I spent a few minutes panting and choking on the cloud of grimy dust I'd raised. After about a thousand rapid-fire blinks, my eyes cleared to the point where I could see again, and I found myself standing amid a heap of jumbled photos. Well, I figured out really fast that I wasn't going to get any guitar practice in, because getting the pictures back into the upside-down box labeled JUDY was going to be a slow process even if I didn't have an asthma attack from the allergen-laden air. I sat down, creating a little secondary mushroom cloud around myself, and started sorting through Solomon Lewis's great disappointment.

An hour later, I was in Sol's room, randomly picking out a sad little blues progression on my Tele — it would have been almost sacrilege to play the down and dirty blues on Sol's D'Angelico, like sketching over the Mona Lisa with watercolors — and trying to process what I'd seen in the "Judy box." It was hard for me to even imagine all the pain Sol had gone through in his life. And the pain was going to get worse before it was through. When they wheeled him in, Sol's skin was the shade of ashes in oatmeal, and his chest looked all puffed up. He grinned at me, but distantly, and you could just tell that it cost him some effort somehow.

His voice was breathy and scratchy at the same time.

"So, *boychik*, what's with the blues? Is that mean old no-good Mrs. Um doin' you wrong again?"

"No, just thinking. How are you feeling? You look tired."

"Well, you know, I have my good days and my . . . not-so-good days. This one isn't necessarily in my top ten."

"Hey, I brought you something." I took out the two huge black-and-white bakery cookies I had stowed under my chair, but he barely even glanced at them.

"Leave them. Maybe I'll . . . be . . . hungry later."

"No problem, Sol. What do you want to work on with me today?"

He was lying all the way back in bed, and while he pondered my question I could hear the air rattling and whistling through his lungs. The guy was suffocating while his genius protégé was offering him cookies. "Like you said, I'm tired right now. Just . . . play something nice. Okay?"

So I played and played: whole songs, half songs, chord progressions, whatever wound up under my fingers. Sol's breathing noises would get louder for maybe a minute at a time, and then so quiet that I almost wanted to stop playing and take his pulse to make sure my playing hadn't carried him off to the Great Beyond. Then at some point, Claudelle came in and stood next to me. She put a hand on my shoulder, and gestured with the other to the doorway. "Come on out, baby," she whispered. "Your friend needs his rest now."

In the hallway, all I could say was, "Why is his chest so loud now? And why does he look all puffed up like that?"

Claudelle sighed before she answered. "Work of breathing, Alex. The doctors call it 'the work of breathing.' You and me, our lungs do all the work the way they should, so it doesn't look hard. But a man like Sol, his lungs are all scarred up and swollen on the inside. So he has to *work* for his oxygen."

"Always? Every breath? Why now?"

"Oh, baby. Your friend in there is a tough old

fighter. But you see how hard it is. And nobody fights forever. Nobody."

I had to get out of there, and I did. I needed Laurie, so I went to her house. Her dad answered the door, and warned me: "Her Highness has retired to her royal bedchamber. She's in a *serious* mood, Alex. She got ultrasound pictures from her mother today, and ripped them into tiny black-and-white confetti. You can go up if you want, but I think I'm just going to stay out of Laurie's way for a while, like, until she turns thirty. I've been hearing sounds, like boards breaking."

"Well, I think breaking her karate boards is a healthy way to get out some aggression, Mr. Flynn."

"So do I, Alex. I just wish she *had* some karate boards at home."

"Oh. Uh, well, I guess I'll be going up the stairs now."

"All right, son. Just in case things don't go . . . well up there, let me just take this time to tell you what a great kid I think you were — I mean, are."

Is the guy just a total riot, or what?

I listened outside of Laurie's door for a few minutes, and couldn't hear any blatantly dangerous noises, so I knocked. She grunted something, which I took as an invitation, and I entered the Chamber of Raging Sorrow. The room was definitely trashed, but I ignored the wreckage, or at least the nonhuman wreckage. Laurie was curled up on her bed with a wad of tissues in one hand and a folded paper in the other. She wasn't actively crying, but she was still in that sniffly post-weep stage. I swept a damp cluster of tissues off the bed onto the floor, and sat by her knees. I gave her one of those weird little pats that old-fashioned country doctors give in the movies when they're delivering horrendous news, and her red-rimmed eyes focused on mine.

"She's really going to have the baby, Alex. She's really going to spawn. Look at this!" She unfolded the paper, and waved it in my face. It was the ultrasound photo her dad had mentioned.

"Hey, your father told me you ripped that up."

"He's such an exaggerator. He probably told you I was breaking things up here too, right?"

I took in the dumped drawers, the beauty supplies scattered everywhere, and the massive diagonal crack in her headboard. I raised an eyebrow.

"Well, he exaggerated about the stupid paper, anyway. I only ripped up the envelope and the cute, annoying card she sent."

I grabbed the ultrasound picture, which basically looked like a radar image of a space alien. The odd being had a gigantic head, a teeny body, little floppy arms and curled-up legs. And, looking more closely, I couldn't help but notice that it appeared to have a tail.

"Whoa," I exclaimed, "Monkey city!"

"Must be from the father's side of the family."

I twisted over Laurie and looked down at her back. "Yup, you appear to be tail-free."

"Thanks for noticing."

Suddenly I couldn't be on the bed, so I started pacing — which was tricky in a room that was maybe eight feet long and had random objects covering its floor to varying depths. "So, uh, you're pretty upset, I guess. But why now? You've known this was coming."

"I know, it's just . . . the picture and the card make it so *real*. Like this new person really is going to come, and be my half sister, and my mother's whole daughter, so I'll be just her half daughter."

"Uh, Laur, remember how I beat you on the math PSAT? I think the logic section may have been your downfall."

"Uh, Alex, remember when we were eleven, and you tried to blow up that huge anthill with firecrackers, and all the ants landed on you, and they bit you everywhere, and you were in the hospital for three days? Don't talk to me about logic, buster!"

"Okay, first of all, that would have worked if the Raid can had just detonated on time. But anyway, all I'm saying is that you're still your mom's whole daughter. Look, she invited you to stay there this summer, right? Doesn't that tell you anything?"

"Yeah, it tells me she's seen *Cinderella*, and she knows cheap labor when she sees it. Maybe I just won't go at all."

"I don't know, Laur. It seems to me like she's reaching out to you. Don't you think that might just burn your bridges with her completely?"

"Maybe I *want* to burn my bridges with her. That way she can't keep jerking me around like this for years at a time!"

She kicked her headboard rather mightily to emphasize her point, and also succeeded in emphasizing the titanic crack in the wood. I strode over to her, insofar as it was possible to stride under the conditions, and put my hand on her shoulder. Her eyes had that little prism thing going, where the tears are just brimming up but not yet running over. We didn't say anything for a long time, until finally I started feeling too nervous with the silence.

"You know, I just think a child and a parent should speak with each other, that's all."

She just stared, so I filled the convo gap again. "I went to Sol's today, and he . . . he wasn't around, so I was in the locker. You know, where I got the guitar from? Because I was going to take it out again and play. But then I knocked everything over — well, I caught the guitar, but — and a box of pictures and stuff fell out. So I was putting them back in, and they were of Judy, his daughter. And she hasn't spoken to him in forever, but he has EVERYTHING of hers in there. I mean, there was a baby tooth in there, and her second-grade report card, and even some news clippings from her grown-up life. And you can just tell he loves her so much . . . but he can't . . ."

Suddenly there were four welling-up eyes in the room. Laurie asked, "How's he doing? What's wrong?"

So I told her what Leonora had said, and Claudelle, and about the horrible noises in his lungs, and how he hadn't even wanted the cookies, even though he had practically twisted my arm to make me bring them. And by then I was completely crying, and so was Laurie, and we were practically swimming in a sea of freshly utilized tissues. Then we were on the bed, and my arms were around her, and hers were around me, and there was a whole long interval of progressively closer eye contact. So we both started leaning in for real, and I could tell this was going to be the big kiss, because I was so sad and so happy at the same time. And I closed my eyes and waited for the gentle brush of her lips on mine . . .

And then there was a tremendous *CRACK*, like a gunshot. I mean, not like some tiny little .22 caliber jobbie either, but like a crazy huge hand cannon from an ultra-violent military-type movie. And Laurie and I tumbled into each other, and we banged teeth AGAIN.

We were on the mattress, which was on the floor, because Laurie's entire bed frame had split down the middle where she'd kicked it. I suppose I recovered first. "Wow, Laurie, you sure do rock at karate!"

She grinned at me adorably through her split lip. "Wow, Alex, you sure do have slick man moves!"

I should write this stuff down some day. But honestly, who on God's green earth would believe it?

PEACE IN MY TRIBE

All the way home from Laurie's house, I thought about two things: my painful, swelling upper lip and my relationship with my parents. If I could cry over Sol's estrangement from his daughter, and if I could tell Laurie to bury the hatchet with her mother, then maybe there were some things I should say to my mom and dad so I didn't have to walk around knowing I was the world's largest hypocrite.

They were sitting at the table, having a late-night cup of herbal tea. It was a scene so normal that I could barely comprehend how a year and a half of insanity could have crept in since the last time I had seen my parents do this. I put a hand on each parent's shoulder. "Mom, Dad, there's something I want to talk to you about."

My father looked worried, so I continued. "Relax, I didn't smash up anybody's car this time. And I'm not failing my classes, and I didn't get anybody pregnant. Or pawn my guitar for crack money. Or . . ."

Mom was sort of laughing, but she squeezed my hand. "We get the point, Alex. So what DO you want to tell us?"

"Well, I was at Sol's tonight, and he's not doing well, and I found a box of old pictures and stuff of his daughter, the . . . his daughter, Judy. So I was thinking about how much he's done for her, and how she doesn't appreciate it. And I know I've been — uh — not so easy with the whole divorce thing. I think you may have noticed."

Mom wasn't going to let that opening pass her by. "Oh, so the whole lawn-gnome incident would have been kind of, oh, I don't know, an anger thing?"

Dad took a shot, too. "And that whole not-talking-to-my-father-for-months routine, would that have been part of a larger pattern?"

"Look, you are both just a raging hotbed of wit, okay? Yes, you both know how angry I was. And how weird it is for me now, to see you back together, only not ALL the way back together. Plus, even if you, like, remarry or whatever, I don't know how I'll ever really be sure it's permanent again."

They shared a pretty awkward little glance over that bit, but I needed to continue.

"But I know you both love me, and I love both of you. I'm sorry if I've been a problem. That's all."

"Problem?" Dad asked. "Did you notice a problem with the boy, honey?"

"No, no problem," Mom replied. "I might have maybe encountered an *issue* or even a *situation*, but not a *problem*, per se."

My mom stood up and hugged me then, and my dad got his arms around both of us. It was weird, because we hadn't necessarily been such a big huggy kind of family before. But it felt good, too. Then Mom broke the mood. "Okay, boys, some of us have a twelve-hour shift tomorrow. I have to get to bed."

Dad asked me if I wanted a cup of tea, and I said yes, even though I secretly think herbal tea tastes like fermented dishwater. When all the shuffling around the kitchen was done, and we were sitting side by side at the table, Dad had something to get off his chest. "Alex, remember when I told you that I didn't run out on Mom, that *she* told *me* to leave?"

I took a long sip of my tepid and yucky beverage. "Yeah?"

"I think maybe I should tell you about what happened between your mother and me last year."

I took another sip, stalling for time while I considered this. "You know what, Dad? I don't really want to know. You gave me enough of an answer in December."

"Really? What did I say?"

"You told me, 'Things aren't so simple. People are complicated and contrary.' And you were right. And that's all I need to know. Really."

Dad looked relieved. "Well, all right, if you're really okay with all this now."

"I am, Dad. I really am."

He started to get up from the table, and it occurred to me that I did have one other question. "Wait. I do have just one more thing I'm curious about, since you asked."

"Okay, shoot."

"Uh, why did you break up with Mrs. Simonsen?"

"I don't know, bud. I just couldn't see spending the rest of my life with a woman who smelled like chalk."

Yes, friends, that's right: Another marriage saved by chalk dust.

April 3

Dear Judge Trent,

This letter has two purposes. The first is to inform you that I feel I have nearly met the requirements of my pretrial intervention assignment. I have now worked over a hundred hours at the Egbert P. Johnson Memorial Home for the Aged. Additionally, and perhaps more important, I think I have learned and applied a life lesson.

The lesson I learned was taught to me by an old man, a vase of flowers, and a box of old mementos. Do you remember how I wrote in an earlier letter that Solomon Lewis has a daughter who doesn't speak with him? Well, he leaves her these flowers every year at Hanukkah time, even though she never comes to get them. Also, he has this storage locker at the home, and I came across a big box of photos and things, labeled "Judy." Of course, he has all of her childhood stuff, like report cards and baby teeth. But he also has a bunch of news articles and things about her adult life that he has found and saved over the many years since their estrangement began. Even with all of the difficulties he has, even though he is terminally ill, he keeps track of his child. It's like, if Sol's daughter would show up, even after all this time, he would be totally ready to pick right up with her again. So the lesson Sol has taught me is this: Most parents love their children, no matter how mad the children get, no matter what the children do or say. Most parents love their children, and everybody deserves a second chance at happiness.

So I told my best friend, who has a very messy relationship with her mother, to give daughterhood another try. And then I went home and put my money where my mouth is: I forgave my parents for their marital problems. Wow. I probably deserve some sort of juvenile delinquent merit badge.

The other purpose of this letter is to invite you to

what will probably be Sol's last concert. His emphysema has taken a bad turn, but he insists on going through with one more jazz performance at the home, this Saturday at three P.M. in the home's rec room. The performance will be really special, because first of all, Sol recently gave me a very valuable and exquisite-sounding jazz guitar, and this will be my first gig with the new instrument. Also, Sol has been giving me guitar lessons for six weeks, and he is an incredible teacher. Plus, he and the other two musicians from my last concert are all brilliant players. So this concert should be a great event musically.

I almost didn't invite you to this event, because you didn't attend the first one. However, as Sol has taught me, we all deserve a second chance!

I hope to see you there.

Alex Gregory

April 6

Dear Alex,

   I will attend.

Sincerely,

Judge J. Trent

FINALE

Imagine this: You are a musician. Not a bad musician, but also not a supernaturally great one. You find yourself on a stage in front of a couple hundred people, many of whom you know personally — and one of whom could theoretically send you to jail if your playing is TOO horrendous. You look around the stage and take in the view of your fellow instrumentalists: the teenage drum wizard looking calmly explosive in khakis and a white button-down shirt; the high school priestess of the piano, clad in a silky-looking dress, cracking her knuckles in a way that is somehow ladylike when she does it; the elderly grand master of all things guitar, looking dapper in an ancient checkered tan blazer with lapels like highway on-ramps. And you try to forget your nervousness and the fact that you are unquestionably the smallest gun up there — that even though you have been working at this harder than you've ever worked at anything, any one of these people could blow you off the stage faster than you can say, "Bebop!" Plus, there are three of them.

You think back to a time when you didn't have to be on this stage, when the throngs weren't all massed in front of you, watching your every move. A simpler time, a quieter time. A time twenty-five minutes earlier, when you were sitting around talking with your bandmates in a little back room.

"Uh, guys, I'm nervous."

"Why?" asked Annette, as she sat holding hands with Steven. "We did a concert just like this one just a couple of months ago."

"I know, but back then, I thought playing well meant just getting through the songs. This time, you guys and Sol have opened me up to vast new horizons of self-criticism."

"But you've been playing great. Really. Steven was just saying last night how far you've come in this short time."

"And it's true. I was telling Annette that you're much more sensitive now. It's like you have a whole new set of ears. Even at the last concert, when you and Annette were both playing accompaniment, you were banging out these huge chords on all six strings, so there wasn't much left for her to play. But two days ago at rehearsal, I noticed on 'I Got Rhythm' that you were only chording on three strings — and it sounded excellent. Plus your strum has gotten a lot lighter and bouncier, too; you've been locking into my beats a lot better."

"Well, that's only because Sol has been yelling at me about that stuff. The other day we were running through the Fiddler medley, and he reached over and started banging on my head in time, shouting, 'Not like that, *boychik*. You sound like a herd of elephants charging through a music store!' The only thing that saved me from permanent brain damage was that he had a big coughing fit and I moved my chair away from the bed before he could recover."

They smiled, and Annette said, "He's really changed you, you know."

"What do you mean? Just because his innovative use of fear as a teaching tool has been . . ."

"No, seriously. You're not just more sensitive as a musician — you're a more sensitive person. Everybody has noticed. Look how you always used to make fun of me and Steven behind our backs."

"Oh, about that. Listen, I just want to . . ."

"See? You were almost going to apologize. A year ago, you would have denied the whole thing, then started making up jokes about us as soon as I stopped talking. Then Laurie would have told me afterward how misunderstood you were, he's a nice guy if you get to know him, blah blah blah. But now you're just, I don't know, better. Nicer."

I could feel the heat of a spectacular blush suffusing my face. I WAS standing there at that very instant, trying to make up a joke or two. But what came out of my mouth was no joke. "Thank you, Annette. Thank you."

Just then, Sol burst into the room in a wheelchair, which was being pushed by a laughing orderly. "Thank you for the ride, my friend. I haven't had that much fun traveling since Rose Friedman took me to the backseat of her Buick in nineteen forty-seven. Hello, kids! I hope you all brought your playing fingers with you today, because this is going to be GREAT!"

He was all rigged up with dual air tanks and a full-face oxygen mask hanging down next to his cannula, which was clipped in place under his nose. Nobody else would be able to play even "Mary Had a Little Lamb" with all this equipment strapped to their head, but this was Sol. Still, his color was horrible, and his voice was ragged. He looked for a moment like he was going to cough, but grabbed the air mask and sucked deeply on it instead.

"Uh, Sol, what's that for? Are you really okay to play?"

He pulled the mask aside a bit. "What — this little thing? I'm fine. I'm just getting ahead on my oxygen." He stopped and took two big puffs from the mask again. "I figure this way, when I stop breathing, I'll have a couple days of life saved up, just in case I'm not done yet!"

Steven and Annette didn't quite know how to take

this, but I knew it meant Sol was going to make it through the day. He was definitely ready for business, too. "Hey, Alex. Are the guitars tuned up?"

"Yes, Sol. They're out there, and Laurie is watching the whole stage while we're back here."

"Good. If that Mrs. Goldfarb gets down here early, there's no telling how much damage she could do with a stage full of instruments. And how is Mrs. Um today? I hope she's not wearing her red dress, or you might have a heart attack and fall off the stage."

"She's wearing jeans, Sol." I put my hand on his. "And you just worry about yourself, okay? I don't want any surprises out there."

"Worry about myself? Why? I'm fine. I've played a million gigs before this one, kid. Nothing can really surprise me onstage anymore. I'm ready for action. You just watch those old ladies checking me out up there, and try to learn a thing or two."

So there I was onstage, twenty-five minutes later, trying to learn a thing or two. We'd played through four tunes, and everybody else was doing their usual top-notch job. Sol wasn't playing the fastest runs I had ever heard from him, but each note was exactly perfect — as though he were carving the melodies into clay tablets so they would last a thousand years. Steven and Annette were just ridiculous — an octopus of rhythm and harmony. As for me, I was mostly just staying out of the way, although I was turning into a fairly accomplished out-of-the-way-stayer, if I do say so myself.

The fifth tune was to be the last one before intermission, and Sol called it: the Fiddler medley, which was my big duet with him. If ever there had been a time for me to screw up on a grand scale, this would have been it. I looked out at the front row, and Laurie was perched on the edge of her seat, chewing her lip — she knew how big this duet was for me, since I had played her my part over and over again for weeks. She gave me a little thumbs-up signal, and I was glad I had her as my supportive whatever-she-was thing. My parents were next to her, happily oblivious, Mom's head on Dad's shoulder. I was glad I had them, and that they were being supportive whatever-they-were things for each other, too. On the far side of my dad was the judge. She had made it!

Sol spoke into the microphone, which some staff member had handed to him while I was staring into space. "Hello. This one is a special song for me. My young protégé here, Alex, will be playing a lot of the melodies. He's worked really hard on the whole thing. He's a good kid. I'd like to dedicate the piece, for both of us, to the lovely girls in the front row."

He counted us in, and we played. At this point, I honestly can't remember anything about how most of the medley went. I must have played it, because we got to the last part somehow. But that part was so mind-blowing that it has wiped out everything else from my memory.

Now, in the fifteen or so times that Sol and I had run through this number, and in the hundreds of run-throughs I had done at home, I always played just the chords for "Sunrise, Sunset" while Sol played the melody. This time, I got through the little intro part, and when it was time for Sol to come in, my eyes were closed in concentration. But his guitar didn't come in. His VOICE did:

> *Is this the little girl I carried?*
> *Is this the little boy at play?*
> *I don't remember growing older,*
> > *When did they?*

> *When did she get to be a beauty?*
> *When did he grow to be so tall?*
> *Wasn't it yesterday when they were small.*

> *Sun-rise, sun-set, sun-rise, sun-set,*
> > *Swiftly flow the days;*
> *Seedlings turn overnight to sun-flow'rs,*
> > *Blossoming even as we gaze.*

> *Sun-rise, sun-set, sun-rise, sun-set,*
> > *Swiftly fly the years;*

One season following anoth-er,
Laden with hap-pi-ness . . . and tears . . .

Claudelle was standing next to Sol, holding the microphone in front of his mouth. I went with the flow, played my parts, and tried to be as quiet and unobtrusive as possible so everyone would hear Sol's voice, which sounded tremendously fragile. At some point, I noticed that the microphone was actually shaking: Claudelle was crying. Anyway, we got through the song, and when the last note faded, Sol immediately grasped for his air mask. There was no applause at all, just total awed silence.

And the judge was walking toward us, with her face behind her hands. She was crying, too. When she was about a foot away from Sol, she leaned over him and said one word, which got picked up loud and clear by Claudelle's microphone:

"Dad."

Sol had the strangest expression behind his mask. "Judy."

CODA

Boop. *Boop. Boop.*

I'm sitting next to the old man's hospital bed, watching the bright green line spike and jiggle across the screen of his heart monitor. Just a couple of days ago, those little mountains on the monitor were floating from left to right in perfect order, but now they're jangling and jerking like maddened hand puppets.

I know that sometime soon, the boops will become one long beep, the mountains will crumble into a flat line, and I will be finished with my work here.

I will be free.

You're probably wondering what happened in the second half of the concert, whether Sol and the judge reconciled, and how we got here. But the truth is, those aren't the most important parts of the story. Of course Sol and his daughter made up, and she visited him daily for two weeks straight, and they talked for hours on end, and laughed a lot, and cried a bunch, too. She also talked a lot with me, and told me how my mom had pulled a "Gotcha" on her by getting me assigned to Sol, of all people. And then one day, we were sitting in Sol's room — me, Laurie, Sol, the judge, and Mrs. Goldfarb, who was stopping in regularly now that Sol was a "star." Just sitting there, just talking. Sol sneezed, then sneezed again, and coughed one short little bark. Then he looked around at all of us and said, "Pneumonia. Get the nurse."

We did, and it was. They took him over to the hospital right away, but you could just tell it was already too late — that this was *it*, the end, circle-the-wagons time. Within a few hours, he had a high fever, his breathing sounded like he was underwater, and he couldn't really do anything but cough. They put the mask on him full-time, and gave him IV antibiotics and painkillers galore. But he was too tired, simply too tired. I remembered Claudelle saying, "Nobody fights forever. Nobody." I sat there, and tasted my tears on my tongue, and watched Sol sleep until they kicked me out for the night.

In the next three days, which were also the past three days, Sol only woke up twice. A doctor told me and the judge that terminal emphysema patients almost always sank into a coma at the end, that this was nature's way of making the end easy. It didn't always look easy, though. Sometimes Sol would just lie there, slumped all the way down, panting. Other times he'd stop breathing for a moment, and then take a series of huge gasps. Once he quickly sat straight up, looked at the judge, and said, "Hey, Judy, you think I could get maybe a cup of coffee in this dive?" in a totally normal Sol voice. Then he slumped over again.

And about an hour ago, Sol turned on his side, right in the middle of a gasping fit, opened his eyes, and peered at the judge. "Be happy, Judy. I loved your mother, and we both loved you. I'm very proud of my girl." Then he locked eyes with me and Laurie. "You're good kids. Alex, *boychik*, one day you will kiss her. And she will kiss you back. Am I right?" When he laid himself back again, we thought he was finished, that all we could do was sit there and cry.

But then he opened his eyes again and gave me some parting advice, his last words on this earth: "*Boychik*, when you finish playing a gig, wipe your strings down with a soft cloth. They'll last longer."

That was it. That was all.

And now the monitor is going nuts, and soon I'll be free. But I guess somewhere in the course of this weird year — my junior year of high school, my senior year of childhood, Sol's last lap around the sun — I figured out that we're all free, in the only way that matters anyway. We're all free to choose some people to love, and then do it.

THE SAINTS GO MARCHIN' IN AGAIN

I have one last thing to do for Solomon Lewis before I can let him go. We're at his memorial service, back at the home, in our little concert hall. The judge — who now insists I call her Judy — has asked me to end the festivities with a guitar rendition of "Taps." I get there early, pull the stage curtain across in front of the piano, do some other setting up, pick a seat in the front row, and wait for all the people to come in. Claudelle is there, Leonora, Juanita. Mrs. Goldfarb — teeth, wig, and all. My parents. Laurie. The judge. Steven and Annette. The oxygen guy. The clarinet player from All-City Jazz Band.

They all sit down, and all the talking happens. There's a podium in front of the stage curtain, and various people use it. I'm sure the speeches are very nice, very appropriate, very touching. I'm also sure that if Sol were here, he'd be saying, "What a load of *chazzerai*! Who wants to hear this stuff now that I'm DEAD? Get out of here, go eat some babka or

260

something!" Finally Laurie is squishing my hand in her deadly Ninja claw grip, and I realize they have called my name. I walk up to the single chair set up to the right of the podium, whisper to the orderly who has been waiting by the stage for this, and get comfortable with Sol's — my — D'Angelico. And then, as slowly as I can, with almost no swing to it whatsoever, I play the tune:

> Day is done, gone the sun,
> From the lake, from the hills, from the sky;
> All is well, safely rest, God is nigh.

I don't look up, but I can hear three sets of footsteps approaching and then passing behind me. When I get to the last note, I hold it out as long as I can with vibrato, mentally thanking Sol for teaching me the trick. And while I'm wiggling that left third finger to keep the sound alive, the orderly opens the curtains. Steven and Annette are there, with drums and piano at the ready. So is the clarinetist, and he jumps in first. I play the sad, sad chords of "Sunrise, Sunset" under his lead, and in the middle I look up. We're wiping everybody out here. The whole first three rows are crying openly; Leonora is handing a tissue to Juanita, who is leaning on Claudelle. And the judge — forget about it. Mascara stripe city. We get to the last note of THAT.

And I say, "One-two-three-four!" We burst into "When the Saints Go Marchin' In." Steven is swinging like there's no tomorrow, Annette is playing such dirty barroom piano that you almost want to blush, and I'm playing chords on three strings, just like Sol would have wanted — I can almost feel his callused palm smacking the beat out on top of my head. The clarinet guy plays through the melody once pretty straight. We go back to the top, and he plays it really funky. Back again, and this time Steven and Annette are trading four-bar phrases back and forth with each other. I look up, and see that we've got the New Orleans vibe going strong. The tears are drying, smiles are coming out, and some feet are even tapping around the room. We repeat the head of the tune once more, while Steven is in full flow,

I'm throwing phrases back and forth with Annette's right hand, and the clarinet is sailing over all of us, maybe all the way to Sol's *new* home.

> *Oh, when the Saints   (Oh, when the Saints!)*
> *Go marching in   (Go marching in!)*
> *Oh, when the Saints go marching in,*
> *I'd like to be in that number,*
> *When the Saints go marching in!*

We stop. The applause is deafening. I mean, people say that all the time, but in this case, it's literally true. Laurie is out of her seat, and my parents and the judge are headed my way, too. I look up at the ceiling, picture what's beyond it, shake my fist once upward in triumph, and say it under my breath: "Gotcha!"

June 27

Dear Judge, or Judy, even though that still feels weird to me,

I know you took some time off from work, and I wanted you to have a letter when you came back from wherever you went. So I'll update you on some things, notably my future.

I got my SAT scores back right after the memorial service, and did quite well on the tests. So I shouldn't have any trouble getting into a great college. I may sell your father's guitar at some point to pay for some of the education I need, or maybe — just maybe — I can keep it and gig my way through school. I have been practicing a ton, because when I play I feel like my friend Sol is there. So my chops are up, and anything is possible. Steven and Annette even keep giving me brochures for music schools!

My parents are looking more and more like they will marry each other again, which would be great. But whatever happens, happens. Each of them has been amazingly there for me this month, and I will be there for them if and when they ever need me.

Laurie's mother had her baby the last week of school, and Laurie went down to help out for a few weeks. We talk pretty much every day, and Laurie sounds like she's doing well there. She even found out her stepdad used to do karate, so she's been getting him to spar with her a little, the poor man. I miss her, but I have a feeling we will be in each other's lives for a good long time.

As for my summer plans, I have decided to work full time at the Home. It's not the same without Sol there, but I've grown close to some other residents and staff, which has been very rewarding. Plus, the pay is good, so I will be able to sock money away into my "car & college fund."

Besides, somebody has to make sure Mrs. Goldfarb keeps her teeth in her head.

Love,

Alex

THANK-YOU NOTES FROM THE MIDNIGHT WRITER

You know that old saying about how "When the student is ready, the teacher appears?" I must have really been primed for instruction during the writing of this book, because amazing teachers popped up right and left.

Interestingly, my most crucial teachers were, and are, my students at Phillipsburg Middle School. I got the idea for this novel from the antics of my morning English class of 2003–04. Then Mrs. Marlene Sharpe's afternoon class served as my inspiring and insightful first audience; I read the manuscript to them aloud as I went along. Last year my students gave me some great revision hints, and several classes this year were extremely helpful in rejecting the eight million lousy titles I went through on the road to finalizing this one. Seriously, if you spent any time in a classroom with me over the past three years, THANK YOU for your great contribution to both this book and my life.

This book also benefited from the advice of three experts. My best friend from middle school and sleep-away camp, Jeremy Stein, Esquire, talked me through the process of a typical juvenile arrest. A local pulmonologist, Dr. John Kintzer, gave me an excellent clinical overview of the progression of emphysema. My friend Karen Sickels spoke with me at length, very graciously, of the experience of watching a loved one die of emphysema. I added my own misinterpretations and outright mistakes, and the results are in your hands.

My editor at Scholastic, Jennifer Rees, was endlessly helpful, instructive, enthused, and available. Come to think of it, so was EVERYONE at Scholastic. I am truly blessed to have wound up at such a wonderful publishing house. Which reminds me of how lucky I am to have my agent extraordinaire, Mr. A. Richard Barber. Thanks for building me a career, Rich.

My final thanks must be reserved for my family. My mom, Dr. Carol Sonnenblick, loved this book, and provided its first "buzz" by passing a manuscript to everyone she knew. My sister and brother-in-law, Lissa and Neil Winchel, both read the manuscript in one night, while I interrupted them every few minutes to say, "Did you like that part? Pretty good, right?" And they didn't even yell at me for being so irritating. My wife, Melissa, and our children, Ross and Emma, lived with me through the writing and revision processes. For all the times I was growly and unavailable, thanks for not chasing me about the house with a flyswatter. I love you.

My late father and head cheerleader, Dr. Harvey I. Sonnenblick, deserves his own paragraph. Dad, you

believed in this book. Whenever something great happened for my first novel, you always said, "You think this
is something? Just wait until the NEXT one comes out!"
I love you, I miss you, and I wish you had waited too.

Bethlehem, Pennsylvania

2006

About the Author

Jordan Sonnenblick attended amazing schools in New York City. Then he went to an incredible Ivy League university and studied very, very hard. However, due to his careful and well-planned course selection strategies, he emerged in 1991 with a fancy-looking diploma and a breathtaking lack of real-world skills or employability.

Thank goodness for Teach for America, a program that takes new college graduates, puts them through "teacher boot camp," and places them at schools with teacher shortages around the country. Through TFA, Mr. Sonnenblick found his place in the grown-up world, teaching adolescents about the wonders and joys — the truth and beauty — of literature.

Mr. Sonnenblick's first novel, *Drums, Girls & Dangerous Pie*, was published by Scholastic Press in 2005 to great acclaim and was named to several Best of 2005 lists, including the American Library Association's Teens' Top Ten.

In October 2006, Scholastic released Mr. Sonnenblick's second young adult novel, *Notes from the Midnight Driver*. It has received starred reviews from *Publishers Weekly*, *Booklist*, *KLIATT*, and *The Horn Book*. Mr. Sonnenblick's third novel, *Zen and the Art of Faking It*, will be published by Scholastic Press in October 2007.

Mr. Sonnenblick lives in Bethlehem, Pennsylvania, with the most supportive wife and lovable children he could ever imagine. Plus a lot of drums and guitars in the basement.

AN INTERVIEW WITH JORDAN SONNENBLICK

Q: *How did you come up with the idea for* Notes From the Midnight Driver?

A: Believe it or not, I was taking a walk one Sunday, and the whole thing popped into my head, pretty much complete. I teach eighth-grade English, and had been really angry with some students in my honors class that week. They had run rampant when I was absent, so I made them write apology letters to my sub and their parents for their behavior. They wrote the most weasely and self-serving excuse notes instead, and the idea came to me: What if a really good kid did something bad, and then refused to take responsibility? The rest just flowed from there.

I ought to go walking more often.

Q: *In the beginning of the novel, Alex gets drunk, steals his mother's car, decapitates a lawn gnome, and gets into a lot of trouble. It's funny, but also very serious. How did you strike a balance between a sense of responsibility and humor?*

A: Well, realistically, you know that a lot of the stupid stuff people do when they are under the influence seems like a great idea to them at the time. So Alex's little automotive voyage had to be amusing from his point of view while it was happening. On the other hand, the morning after can be a horror. So that aspect had to be honest, as well. And, like Judge Trent in the book, I truly hate the very thought of drunk driving.

Q: *Is Alex based on anyone you know?*

A: His personality just kind of came to me, but his situation of watching his parents separate when he's

16 and his devotion to music are both drawn from my life.

Q: *Is Sol?*

A: Oh, yeah! Sol is totally based on my maternal grandfather, Solomon Feldman. Grampa Sol was my hero when I was a kid for his warmth and his fearlessness, but everybody else kind of tiptoed around him because he had quite a temper. He didn't play guitar, though. He was a biologist and teacher, and what he gave to me was a love of science and a passion for teaching kids. Plus maybe a touch of that temper . . .

Q: *Laurie is just about the coolest girl on the face of the planet. How did you end up making her so unique, and just how in the world does she put up with Alex?*

A: You know what? Laurie just came to me fully-formed, like Athena springing from Zeus's forehead.

When I was a teenager, I always had a female best friend. Laurie is a composite of all of them, I think. How does she put up with Alex? I have no idea — I have no clue how my female friends put up with me, either!

Q: *Music is a big part of this book, as it is in your debut hit,* Drums, Girls & Dangerous Pie. *Being a musician yourself, does writing about music come as naturally as playing it?*

A: I find it really hard to write well about the act of playing music, actually. But when I was a teenager, I always wished that someone would write about characters who loved music the way I loved it. So I have struggled to get that love down onto the page — it's my gift to all the kids out there who hang out in the band room until a grown-up makes them go home.

Q: *If readers could only take away one message or idea from* Notes *what would you want it to be?*

A: When you hurt people, suck it up and face what you've done. That's one of the hardest and bitterest lessons in the world, but everybody needs to figure it out at some point.

Q: *Do you have anything personally against lawn gnomes?*

A: Nah. I just find the entire concept of the lawn gnome good for an automatic laugh. Some things are just, you know, funny.

That same day, in social studies, I accidentally added a whole new facet to my pretend identity. Santa Dowd was asking questions about the textbook reading assignment from the night before: "The Spread of Buddhism: China and Japan." Now, admittedly, I hadn't done the reading the night before, but I already knew this stuff. I had even done a whole poster project on Taoism and Zen Buddhism. I've always liked poster projects, mostly because I love the smell of markers.

Even though everyone obviously liked this Dowd guy, of course nobody raised a hand to answer anything he asked. Kids were squirming around, avoiding the dreaded teacher-eye contact, organizing folders, and sharpening pencils that could have already sliced through Kevlar body armor. Woody was looking at me, which caused my big mistake. I wanted to smile at her, but was afraid that would be un-shy of me — so I turned away, right into the twinkly baby-blues of Mr. Dowd. Once he had me in an eye-lock, I knew it was coming. But like a deer in headlights, I was powerless.

"Mister Lee? Can you explain how Buddhism was adopted and adapted in China?"

Huh, I actually did know this. And I was the perfect guy to answer it, since I had been adopted and adapted FROM China. But was I the kind of shy kid who answered teachers' questions, or the kind who crumbled under the glare of full-class scrutiny? Should I mumble "I don't know"? Fall off my chair again? Faint, and hope Woody would seize the opportunity to revive me with mouth-to-mouth?

My eyes flashed over to the new love of my life. She was smiling encouragingly, but didn't necessarily look like she'd be ready to administer CPR if I needed it. So what the heck, I took a stab at answering the question.

"Well, Indian Buddhism was brought to China by traders about, umm, fifteen hundred years ago. The story goes that a man named Bodhidharma was the first Zen master. He and his followers combined the basic ideas of Indian Buddhism with earlier Chinese traditions like Taoism and Confucianism to create Ch'an Buddhism, what the Japanese later called 'Zen.' 'Ch'an' means 'meditation,' by the way."

Had I really just said all that? I guess I had just decided which kind of shy kid to be. I took a breath, looked around, and saw that everyone was looking at me like I had just sprouted a second head. Except Dowd and Woody, who were both smiling. Hmm . . . maybe acting smart had fringe benefits!

Dowd nodded. "Very good, San. Have you . . . uh . . . studied Zen before?"

Whoa. On the one hand, teachers usually avoided the topic of students' personal beliefs like the plague. But on the other, I realized that everyone in the room was probably thinking *Chinese kid = Buddhist.* And Woody was still smiling.

I played it cool. "I guess you could say that." A mysterious and knowing half smile played across my lips. Wow, I had a mysterious and knowing half smile!

The lesson moved on, and I answered a bunch of other questions. Near the end of the period, the angry kid — the LARGE angry kid, in case I forgot to mention it — next to Woody leaned across her and asked me in a booming voice, "So, Buddha Boy, if a tree falls in the forest, and nobody is around to hear it, does it make a noise?"

Now, a normal teacher might have jumped all over this guy for blatantly attacking the new kid. But Dowd just leaned back against the chalkboard and twinkled. I hoped his back was getting smeared with fluorescent chalk. On the other hand, I was pleased to note, Woody looked irritated with the smirk the kid was now sporting.

Shy or not shy, I wasn't going to roll over and turn into some steroid case's whipping boy. I replied quietly, calmly, "If a monkey howls and nobody listens, is he still a monkey?"

There was a beat while everyone processed this. Then an intake of breath, followed by a wave of snickering. Two wimpy-looking guys I recognized from the chess table high-fived in delight. Somebody near the front of the room muttered, "Oh, snap! Jones got *told*!"

Felt pretty good until I caught the expression on Woody's face. Now she looked annoyed with me too.

Everyone was looking back and forth between me and the hulking figure of Jones, wondering whether social studies was about to get interesting. But Dowd stepped smoothly into the silence and assigned a chapter to read for homework. Luckily for me, it was more stuff I already knew. This way, if Jones broke all my fingers right after class, I wouldn't have to try turning the pages with a bulky cast on.

When the bell rang, I took my time packing up my backpack. If I scurried out of the room, I'd look like a coward. Well, I was a coward, but there was no need to advertise it.

A shadow fell over me — a wide shadow. I looked up from my fascinating bag-zipping activities, and Jones was leaning over my desk. His massive, veiny arms bulged with power as he put his weight on them. But his face wasn't in "kill" mode. In fact, he had a sort of rueful grin going. Woody and Dowd, who were the only two other people still in the room, looked on with interest as Jones's growl swept over me: "Good one, Buddha Boy. You're pretty funny."

I tried to paste the mysterious half smile onto my face, but I suspect it looked a little bit sickly as Jones punched me playfully in the arm and walked out of the room.

With Woody. Dang.

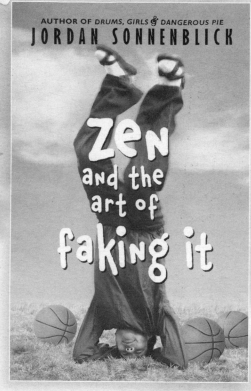

Sometimes the best way to fit in is to stand out.

When San Lee moves to a new town and a new school for the umpteenth time, he devises a plan. This year, he's going to be different, and he's doing it Zen Master–style. But just when he thinks everyone is on to the fact that he's faking it, they start to believe him—in a major Zen way.

SCHOLASTIC

www.scholastic.com

FAKINGI™